OTHER WORK BY SUSAN WINGATE

MYSTERIES
Of the Law (Hard-boiled)

The Bobby's Diner Series (Amateur Sleuth)
Sacrifice at Sea (available November 2013)
Hotter than Helen (Book No. Two)
Bobby's Diner (Book No. One)

YOUNG ADULT ROMANTIC FANTASY BY SUSAN
WINGATE
Susie Speider Books
Ant Brains (March 2014)
Spider Brains (Book One)

Learn more about Susan Wingate books at:
www.susanwingate.com, at Amazon.com, at
BarnesandNoble.com, and in bookstores close to you.

Critical Acclaim

"Labeling Susan Wingate as Chick Lit is akin to accusing Steven King of freelancing for Harlequin! ~Simon Barrett, eBloggerNews

"The narrator's voice is very genuine and compelling. Strong women are always appealing, and these are two very strong women. Wingate develops [the story] with a lovely, light touch... Wingate handles the narrative with such ease. [The reader is] drawn to her honesty. Brava, Susan. ~Phyllis Schieber (author of "The Sinner's Guide to Confession")

"Susan Wingate shows an understanding of human nature well beyond what is normally seen in a novel. She has a mastery of dialogue that I find refreshing—I felt as though I was right there, listening. It isn't often I find dialogue so true-to-life. Between her mastery of dialogue and understanding of human nature, Susan Wingate held me captive... you will find yourself saying "Just one more chapter" over and over again. It is one of those rare books you won't want to put down. I look forward to reading more of Ms. Wingate's work." – Joyce Anthony (author of "Storm" and blog mistress of Books & Authors blog)

2011, 2012, 2013 Copyright © by Susan Wingate

All rights reserved. First printed May 2011

August 2013

Paperback Version 2013, 2nd Edition

ISBN 978-061544812-1

This story is a work of fiction. All characters, names, and events in this book are fictitious. Any resemblance to persons living or dead or real places are purely coincidental.

Cover design by Roberts Press

Book Design by Roberts Press

Edited by Roberts Press

Published by Roberts Press (an imprint of False Bay Books)

685 Spring Street, PMB 161

Friday Harbor, WA 98250

www.robertsbookpress.com

Books are available for special promotions. For details email info@robertsbookpress.com

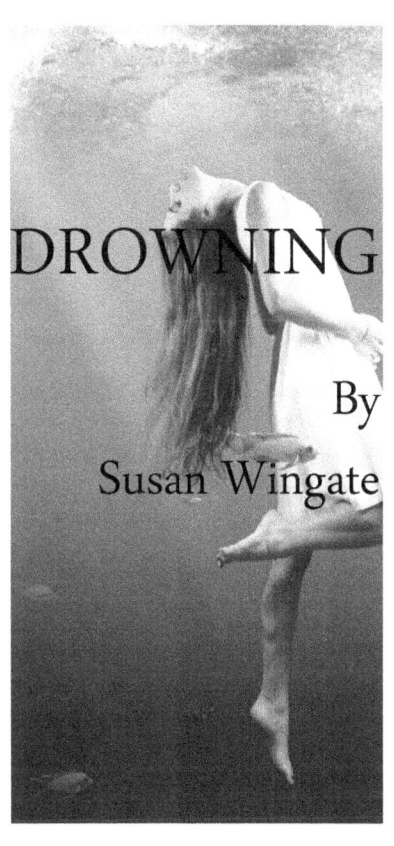

DROWNING

By

Susan Wingate

For
mothers & daughters everywhere
who may not always see
eye-to-eye.

DROWNING

PROLOGUE – CHILD'S PLAY

I took my last breath on a blistering hot day but it felt cool. The second my brother pushed me in, when my feet left the deck, I reacted – my body curving and twisting into correct formation and diving with my fingertips first into the sweet welcome contrast of the pool's frigid water. Young bodies are like that – supple and quick to respond.

He didn't get away with it. He didn't win. See, I decided to play a trick on him for pushing me.

Each millimeter, every dry molecule of my skin became drenched as I dove beneath the surface, deep, deeper to the bottom. I stayed down longer than necessary and the funny thing was? It made me happy down there.

A beating drum pounded my chest with music from the party above and voices sounding like Charlie Brown's cartoon mother saying *wah wah wah*, swallowed up their words and muffled through a filter of water.

After deciding my time spent below had been long enough, I pushed off the scratchy surface of the pool but there were so many people floating, dog- paddling, coursing the length of the pool, re- surfacing, it reminded me of a fantastical dance, maybe one performed only in heaven, hanging over my head. But, I knew I could hold my breath a long time. We had breath-holding-contests in the shallow end of our pool, at home, all the time.

My heart began to race harder from excitement when I noticed the overload of vibrant swim suits, bodies, and legs – the water saturated with color and movement. I felt like I wanted to stay down there forever and the thick thump in my heart continued. Siphoning down, as I sat on the pool's floor, the muffled drumming of music and disguised chatter above me and people, adults and kids alike playing, laughing, living was mesmerizing!

That's when the trick turned on me.

I sort of remember slipping away when that man lifted me up through the water. Then, I saw mother standing beside me, then in front of me as I stood behind her or to the right or left and above her, whichever my new eyes took me. She crumbled. Slumped, over my body that way and cried but it didn't make me sad. It didn't make me feel anything. I just watched. I just watched.

I had been taunting my brother terribly. He was making eyes at a girl there. I jeered and chanted at him, "Two little love birds sittin' in a tree K-I-S-S-I-N-G!"

He yelled for me to stop but I wouldn't and mocked him over and again with my silly song. He turned to me with a raised hand and his face turned beet red. Frozen, waiting for his hand to connect, my eyes got wide--wider than wide. My mouth shut tight waiting for the inevitable slap but then I could see his hand only threatened. He smirked slightly so I said to him, "Why don't you marry her?"

That's when he pushed me. I screamed and giggled and went under. I could see from below that he walked off in the direction of the girl. The water blanketed me. I swam deeper but stopped midway to watch him as he walked to the end of the pool toward the girl. She was sun-bathing on the diving board and he stood over her and placed his hands on his hips then he stuck out one hand for her to shake. When she took it, I spun like a mermaid and dove deeper to the floor. Even down there I smelled the tart burn of chlorine inside my nose.

People jumped in above me. Everything turned into a kaleidoscope of bodies, a ballet. My head began to pound from the pressure. But I stayed just a little longer, five more seconds, I kept saying to myself, just five more seconds.

At home, we used to blow out all of our air to make our bodies sink, so we could sit on the bottom of the pool. What little air was left in my lungs (having performed this stunt many times before), I figured it would be fine. I sat on the drain and watched the show above me. I wasn't down all that long, three minutes, maybe four. That's all.

You know? We're allowed few memories from our time spent on earth. My memories are of the moments before I died, those wavy twinkles, when I was exuberant with joy and of my brother and sister, my mother and father.

I felt doze-y and wanted to come up but the effort of merely standing squeezed my chest. I tried to push off the bottom but rose only a few inches. I had no float! The air was depleted from me and the pool was far deeper than any other I had ever swum in. I tried to rise but realized I might be in for some trouble. I tried to climb a wall but gravity's hands kept holding me down. And, my young arms couldn't reach the ladder when I stretched out, and I stretched.

Energy trickled out of me. My neck and arms ached as though I were carrying an elephant. I tried once more to reach the ladder and it was at that point my body took over. It jerked in odd movements as if I owned it no longer. As my body twisted my legs and arms flailed. My lungs surrendered and I took in my first deep breath. I swallowed too. The water flowed in so easily through my nose, then in past my throat, finally filling my chest. My body convulsed again searching for air and finding none. Once again I sucked in water, swallowed more, and for a mere second I felt fear and, then, all my fear was gone.

I watched my body float aimlessly. It coasted for seconds, with my face pointed toward the floor. It floated like this until the man grabbed me and swam up, lifting me out of the pool.

That was the last time they held one of those big parties, those Maharajans, because of me, because I taunted my brother. It's a shame really.

They'll never understand how happy those last few moments for me were. They'll never understand how beautiful it was to hear people's laughter and singing, to see all those bodies and colors above me, dancing, living! through my water lens.

"Dying is something we human beings do continuously, not just at the end of our physical lives on this earth." – Elisabeth Kubler-Ross

CHAPTER ONE

Why would she lie? Why now, knowing she was going to die?

Somehow Belle's words felt contrived, forced. Euly Winger had been calling her mother Belle since around the age of fourteen. When Belle showed signs that Euly could treat her as an equal.

Her mother's words rung like an indictment, allowing a wisp of a notion making Euly recoil from something that happened long ago, evoking a lingering emotion in Euly, a dreamy memory, caught somewhere between the dead and the living and equally unattainable to conjure.

What was it her mother said? The exact phrase, the exact placement of words, the first one and then the next, that stirred in her such a strong reaction?

"He's your brother." Was it that simple? No, she had added the word "probably" and, with emphasis. Euly remembered how, when Belle spoke, her breath leached out a rancid, metallic odor grown from all the intravenous drugs pumping into her, drugs keeping her alive.

Her veins looked larger against her pale mottled alabaster skin, accenting the clear plastic lines stabbed into her arms, covered by white paper tape to hide where the needles had been inserted.

No. That's not what she said. Belle's exact phrase was, "He's probably your brother." There it was. And Euly's mind roller-coastered back to a spot, an exact time, location, and age--the way the scent of mown grass takes you back in a specific point in your history, to your childhood.

Belle had said it as if to sentence her father, yet again, for their divorce. A divorce that happened so many years ago, a lifetime really, that Euly wondered how it could still bother her mother. But it did.

She stared into her cup dunking her teabag as she tried to put the pieces of yesterday's conversation back in order and wondering if her mother had tasted the hate drooling off of her tongue.

Belle's year-old diagnosis felt like a slap across Euly's face--a swift year that blew by like a fleeting Santa Ana. And, what made it worse? The doctors now gave Belle less than a month. If that.

CHAPTER TWO

Under the quiet blanket of early morning, visions of the past reeled up in foggy fragments from some dusty pigeonhole in Euly's mind. On mornings like these she allowed ghosts to float in and summon up distant scenes. This morning's scene, from some forty years before, was one she'd pressed into a scrapbook — a dried-out rose of a vague history she'd long ago ironed and stowed away, banished, for her own sanity--dragged at her. The corpse, resurrected, felt like a cement block with an anchor chain linking them together, attached to her ankle holding her under water, and keeping her from reaching the surface for air.

Euly sat snugged into an arm of the den's fleecy sofa. In both hands, she hugged her first cup of tea, her ritual. She often sat this way, in the dark of the morning, since she'd moved to the small northwest island, when dull hours hid her and the sun hadn't fully burned through the veil of the waning night.

With a spotlight shining on those living inside the bell jar of her island, Euly existed under the finite walls of a snow globe--that maddening sense of claustrophobia. With waters licking the entire surround of the small lone island and no bridges to connect people who lived there to humanity on the mainland and travel only by boat or plane, Euly felt trapped.

But, why it mattered to her anymore, she wasn't sure since she rarely left. She landed on the tiny islet ten years ago in 1997 when she ran away from the city and her ex-husband. The trade-off had good and bad points. It too came with skeletons.

Like the bungalow outside calling to her. Now, merely a place set aside for houseguests, the cottage stood alone and empty. A stark contrast from before when it was filled with life, art and music, tangled together in a gorge of magic--Belle's home before her exile to the hospice.

Now, only a husk remained--a locust shell--as Belle Masada spent her final days deposited in a place, a terminus, for the sick and dying.

These days the cottage sat dark and barren on their property like stagnant water reminding Euly that time was not in her mother's favor.

With her legs crooked to her chest, Euly kept her feet warm by pulling on the knobby pair of woolen socks she'd left on the ottoman the night before. While she sat in the corner of the sofa next to the red-hot fireplace she remembered, not too long ago the fireplace would've needed a cedar log and stoking but now a simple remote controller kept the gas on and a fire glowing hot.

She gazed into the flame and seemed to melt into the moment with her dog and cat nestled close by.

Outside, birds beckoned to each other in a scurry within the woods. She turned her head from the glow and gazed through the French door's mullioned window to see if she could spot the noisy culprits but the gunmetal gray morning made silhouettes tarnish into colorless shards when she tried to focus her eyes. She noticed how birds of the northwest, seemed fewer in number than in Phoenix.

Three years after the break-up of her first marriage, she'd remarried Geoff Winger. Euly wondered why she had done it. She wondered about it the day of their wedding and now, five years later, their relationship suffered all on its own.

Fearing the marriage would crumble, Geoff had planned for them a stay in Lebanon the coming spring. A gesture to her background, she supposed.

Considering the vacation caused Euly hope and concern all at the same time. The trip, intended to spark some renewed sense of romance, zigzagged between euphoria and dread for her. She loved to say she was traveling to the land of her family's roots but, in the quiet of the morning like now, a dense numbing that hobbled her.

CHAPTER THREE

Geoff burst through the door when he came home that day. He walked up to Euly, wide-eyed, smiling and grabbed her around the waist then gave her an extended kiss.

"Wow. What did I do to deserve that?" It reminded Euly of when he'd gotten up the nerve to ask her to marry him.

They'd talked about a trip but never made any firm plans. The idea hung around them and every once in a while they'd comment, "wouldn't it be nice..." but nothing ever came of it. With Euly's mood becoming darker these days, Geoff had taken a bold step to push forward with the notion and make the idea real.

"What's going on?"

"Well, you know how we've talked about taking a trip..." Geoff looked like he would split at the seams.

"Yes." Her voice swung up in a quizzical manner and she shut off the water she had running. "I did it."

"Did what?" She tried to control her demeanor, her apprehension about his coming declaration.

"I got us two tickets to Beirut. For the spring."

His eyes widened and he frowned when he her face went deadpan. She wanted to recover, make him feel good about his surprise, but she failed him.

"Well, uh, I don't know. I might be busy then."

Geoff tipped his head and squinted in disbelief. His blue eyes seemed to lint over. It was obvious to her he expected Euly to respond differently.

"I thought you wanted to go. We talked about it."

"Oh. Well, yes, I do but I just didn't think it would be so soon."

"Soon? We've been talking about it for five years. Anyway, better now than later, right?"

"Oh, yeah, urn. Oh, shit. Of course, it's okay. I mean, it's great, right?" She hugged him around the neck. "I'm sorry. It's great, really. I guess we'll just have to make plans, now, won't we?"

CHAPTER FOUR

When Euly turned her head back from the chatter of the birds, she caught a faint dank mustiness emanate from around her. The couch was damp to the touch. One of autumn's generous rains, dragged into the house by the animals, had been tracked onto the sofa's jade upholstery and smelled somewhere between wet fur and moldy earth. But, a load of clothes tumbling in the dryer wafted in and balanced out the sofa's bawdy tang. The sofa could wait for cleaning after her morning routine and certainly until the light of day.

Lately, Geoff had taken to complaining about her sloppy habits, the books piled on the wooden floor, the heap of newspapers a foot high on top her desk, and the mountain of laundry waiting to be washed, dried, folded, and put away. Even her library wall looked disheveled. Books she'd read were replaced in careless disarray on shelves, and not properly slotted into each author's spot. After looking around the room, she realized she'd chewed her thumbnail down to a jagged quick — a nasty habit she could barely abide in herself. She examined it and then used the ragged thing to pull a cord of hair behind her ear — another nervous habit. Then, she shoved her hand under her arm to stop all of it.

With fall well underway, she made a silent promise to spend the season becoming more organized, more thoughtful about her husband's wishes. That, of course, meant taking time out of her busy workday – writing obituaries for a mid-size newspaper's online service – to do household chores. Her anger flared when she considered

Geoff's ability to make cleaning and cooking her responsibility alone and not his own. She rolled her eyes and the steaming subsided into a simmer. Anyway, writing obits wasn't exactly what she'd intended when she set off on a career as a writer. The book she'd embarked upon at forty came to a cold stop before it ever got off the ground. Still the idea of writing something longer like a novel tugged at her. And, since her mother's illness turned critical, she contemplated writing a memoir. Although she wasn't clear her motives were pure – if writing the memoir was appropriate in light of her mother's coming death (at which point she could use stories she might not if Belle was still alive).

Even so, she figured the story could be truthful without being cruel and so resolved that now was just as good a time as any. She could squeeze the memoir into her workday even if it meant forgoing an extra load of laundry.

Damn! How did laundry become more important than her own work?

She realized she'd flitted from Lebanon to the laundry within a matter of seconds. Maybe hormones were controlling her feelings this morning. Then she reconsidered. Maybe her mood was the rumbling from some of old history in her life giving way to her emotional unrest.

In a matter of minutes, the day had turned a grizzled haze. She watched a flurry of soft winds sway the trees and imagined herself rocking in a cradle. She wished for a time before, an easier time from her youth.

A remembered dream snuck into her mind from the night before and muzzled Euly's swelling animosity to those things, those people, outside her control. In the dream, her ex-mother in-law, Sharice and she were locked in an embrace and profoundly happy to see one another after so many years. The mirage slid from a dream into a nightmare when she considered some virulent manifestation of her subconscious creating the vision – perhaps some hidden meaning about Belle's deteriorating health. She'd always gotten along well with Sharice but after the divorce from her first husband, she'd lost track of her. So, why then would she let this memory crop up now? Guilt socked her in the gut and shuddered through her body.

Sharice and Belle were vastly different from one another, a Mutt and Jeff of mothers. Euly remembered how they talked together one Christmas. Sharice sat nervously next to Belle who seemed to be conducting her own version of a cross- examination. The only things missing were a hard wooden stool and a flashlight. She remembered approaching the women. Belle's smile appeared trite and fake. Sharice turned her head away. Euly knew by her mother's pinched face, she didn't approve of Sharice. At that point, Euly had pinpointed a disparity. When Belle smiled, she smiled only with her mouth not her eyes.

Euly's tea was still searing hot. She blew on the brew before each sip, trying to divert a sting on her tongue and sucked in cool air along with each thorny snap of bergamot.

Her cat, Raz, jumped onto the arm of the couch where she sat startling Euly back to the present. When she jerked, tea spilled on her sweatpants boiling through to her legs.

"Raz." She squawked quietly pulling up on the hot wet spot and blowing at it.

Finally, Euly stretched out crossing her legs over the ottoman. She patted her lap in a welcome for the cat. The cat coyly placed a single paw on one of Euly's spreading thighs.

The earliest part of mornings were the few hours of the day she didn't mind her recent weight- gain — in the dark, and for the cat. Menopause, so far, had been kind to her. Anyway, she decided, she could use a pound here and there, for the cat, if nothing else.

It wasn't that she was overweight. She just wasn't her prime weight any longer. Her dog, Jonathan, lie quietly next to her and didn't stir, not through the shift of their positions nor through the cat's motor-like-purr drumming like a soft muffled alarm clock stuffed somewhere in a drawer.

Euly sat alone in the fog the morning provided. She wondered if she could ever remember a time when things were happy in her small family. She desperately flipped through pages of her history trying to recount happy moments, if only just one. Her heart pounded as page after troubled page elicited heartache, bitter scenes of accusation, threat and tears. She rubbed her eyes in order to thwart an onset of emotions but already felt a dewy film under her fingertips.

Then, what brought her to this point, returned her yet again when she remembered another childhood memory, the memory of a party and how that party was the last one like it they would ever have.

Her father's family was of Arabic descent and it was this side Euly most identified. The Maharajan was an annual bash. Euly remembered going to several when she was young, but that was a good forty years before. That was when the parties ended too. Euly remembered a younger version of herself then, an innocent version – lost and forgotten – and maybe it was that girl's voice when she heard herself utter a prayerful, *Jesus.*

The day was a Saturday, a morning one summer during the middle 1960s. At Maharajans, people of Middle Eastern descent – and for Euly, Lebanese people – reconnected, caught up on lives, and felt some sense of unanimity in their heritage. People met, laughed, sang, danced, and gossiped.

Belle, fair-skinned and blonde, went along to these parties out of marital obligation. Others thrilled to join in the times meant for heritable camaraderie.

Everyone drank punch or beer, if old enough. People ate, drank and sang by a deep winking pool that seemed to laugh.

By shaking her head, Euly tried to derail the memory and where it would end, but it didn't work. She understood these early morning hours were saved for past acquaintances, those tortured visions of life we stuff under a rug and then shake out when the filth reaches a critical point. Euly winced at the metaphor, how a dirty rug might relate to her past.

Still, Euly let the vision of the pool ebb out and return. The cool offender, adorned with sapphire tiles demarcating a high fill-line and ochre-stained cool deck from years of dirty feet on it, summoned its visitors.

Aunt Moon's son was there, Micaiah. He had he showed her how to roll her towel in order to carry it under one arm instead of holding it awkwardly in front of her like a doll at her chest while she walked. He was the closest thing she had to a brother. Anyway, he felt like a brother. She was only six-years-old at the time and small for her age. She remembered bouts with allergies and a variety of illnesses that kept her body from growing. Like that old cartoon character she recalled, an alligator — a sadly distorted fellow — only its large head scene out of the water swimming across a river. He crawls out and reveals a comparatively tiny body. The alligator then looks straight into the camera to explain his odd shape and says I've been sick. Somehow Euly identified with the sickly alligator but Micaiah did a great thing when he showed her how to roll her towel. He made her feel normal.

Euly staved off the memory a few seconds longer by looking out toward the lighting sky. The tea's scent taunted her senses and helped yank her back into the present. She dragged in another deep breath and held it for a second before shooing Micaiah out of her mind. A thin line in the East's horizon meant only minutes until dawn.

However, when she turned her head back, she was with Micaiah.

He was about ten, a year older than Enaya, Euly's sister. He was a big brown boy with thick black whorls of hair. Yet, Euly couldn't help going back to that day at the Maharajan.

The day sweltered. The sizzling blacktop glistened from heat. The shiny tar softened under their feet when Micaiah, Enaya, and Euly ran from the broiling car toward the coolness of the hall inside. The party was already under way.

A sense of great promise bubbled up in Euly, especially when she thought about the crystalline water of the pool. Ready for a swim, she and her sister donned bathing suits showing-off shapeless fledgling bodies –

tube-like figures of childhood, lean legs prickled with blonde peach-soft hair, red and tanned skin, and Micaiah in his boy swim trunks and round barrel chest.

They wore faded, yellow rubber thongs on their small feet.

The exact point in time?

When thongs were made of flimsy rubber. When the Beatles and Frank Sinatra mixed into a medley of songs. When vendors drove in lazy vans through the neighborhoods playing plunky ice cream tunes. And, when a quarter bought a 50-50 bar.

Euly's dad and Uncle Teddy hurried into the party even before the kids. Mother and Aunt Moon lagged behind gathering up picnic items they'd brought along for the family. Euly fumbled with the towel and that's when Micaiah helped her.

She stared in awe at the beauty of the resort.

With its yucca framed gardens, saguaro cactus and bright berried prickly-pear, the choky fragrance of mesquite trees intermixed with pungent chaparral, and rosy bougainvillea dripping from a high white jagged stucco wall, a wall that surrounded the resort's Olympic-size pool where the festivities took place, by the edge, just a toe-in away.

All the laughter screeched to dead silence when a woman screamed her daughter's name — a scream that ended the morning. Time staggered like a skip in an old scratched record. Sound faded into beats, a muffled footfall of bare feet coming to a standstill. Then, there was no sound, only a poisoned hush — the kind of hush when a cuckoo strikes one — when movement and breathing altogether stop. And, it all takes place in the time it takes a hummingbird wing to flutter just once. Then, a slow rumble buoyed up in a swell flowing up and over the crowd watching — a rumble of whispers. She's only five someone said. As if five had some special meaning. As if five was the determining point of swimming or drowning. As if five meant she shouldn't die.

Then, someone said the girl was her cousin yet even back then Euly couldn't remember her eyes or smile. She couldn't remember running fast with her on slippery concrete that hemmed the pool's water or running by signs that warned NO RUNNING. She couldn't remember slapping patty- cake-hands with mirrored faces beating out the words to Baker Man. Things cousins should remember. Then people began to move again but this time in slow-motion. Their heads their faces locked in statements of wonder, shock, torture.

Their movement all slowed down as if the world itself had stopped spinning that very second. But, in the very next heartbeat, time sped up again. People's heads turned fast. Their wet hair slapping faces in quick snaps. They finally paid attention long enough to see why the woman was screaming, what all the fuss was about. And, then everyone realizing in unison, the girl there, still arms and legs splayed out comfortably as the rocking water moved her body softly along the bottom of the pool. People stood idly by watching as if it were a street show.

That's when someone moved. A man dove in. She couldn't recall his face but he dove deep and stayed under for a terribly long time, if only in seconds.

Then, Euly stopped in a jolt. Amid all the fun, the singing, the laughter, the swimming, she couldn't recall the lemony tabouli she must've eaten or the chalky paste of chickpeas in the hummus. She didn't remember the boozy licorice nip of Arak her father, Ray, always let her sip, or dancing with him. She didn't remember other kids' laughing faces or jokes, or the music blaring over a clamor of voices. She didn't even remember the stink of chlorine that must have smothered the air. What she remembered was the keen sense of panic and sudden quiet.

Euly's hand covered her mouth when her memories took her to the drowning. Phoenix, a burgeoning southwestern desert town, that looked more like an oasis back then than the sprawling metropolis it was today. She could still feel the sun burning her skin even ten years after she'd stolen away to the cooler climate of Washington. The oasis had long since dried up and grown into just another big city where one town encroaches onto the next, another encroaches onto it, and another, and goes on like this past the city boundaries until you can't tell where one line ends and the other begins. Squalor found in every large metropolis had found its way there too. Crime, smog, back-to-back traffic, toxic garbage-can-lined streets, the indigent, the transient, a floundering ghetto but Phoenix had heat to boot, a daunting and oppressive heat.

Euly knew the heat drove the little girl into the pool at that last Maharajan. Yet, everyone at one time or another jumped in to enjoy its sweet coolness. They did to get out of the tireless never- ending sun. The girl who drowned was no different from any other child there that day. The water looked cool and quenching. Kids already in the pool bobbed above the water-line like apples in a barrel. Others swam like tadpoles from one long end to the other. No problem.

Aunt Moon had told the family another horrific morsel of information surrounding the girl's drowning. The girl's parents also lost their youngest son only a few years prior. They'd relocated from Ohio to Phoenix because of it. Their youngest boy himself had drowned in a cistern at a nearby farm. As kids will during a summer heat wave, they found a swimming hole. Euly could only imagine the depth of pain felt by the parents that day. She couldn't grasp the lopsided fate the universe had handed this single family. She thought how one child dying from drowning is surely the limit for any family and, yet, they drew another losing card.

Euly remembered the vastness of that day, at the beginning of it. She pictured the events in broad terms but only moments later, the day was brought into surgical view as if watching it on a homemade movie.

People mingled. A group of older gents danced the dubke, a line dance her people had brought with them from the old country. A couple of old men played the tablahs and bendirs – bongo- like instruments wrapped in dried goatskin for the drumming surface. Old women behind them sang in warbled melodies that swung from soprano to alto like a wild rollercoaster, and twisted their hands and moved their bodies in a slow rhythmic gyration to the men's music. These scenes were sketchy as if Euly might be making them up for effect.

But she hadn't made-up the vision of that woman, the mother, shrieking as she tore through the crowd. When she noticed, she nearly knocked down another lady in a hurry past to get to her daughter. Her voice, wretched and guttural, wailed as if a fox caught in a trap.

That's when the man jumped in. The mother crumbled to her knees at the edge of the pool and waited there on the hot decking. She groaned out a muddle of words while her body rocked and swayed above the water line. She pressed her hands so hard into her mouth that it seemed to freeze her face into a scream.

Her moaning and rocking continued until the man swam up with the girl's limp body in his arms. He had little trouble lifting her small drenched frame out of the water. As the child lie motionless in front of this woman, she seemed unsure of what to do with her hands. They hovered over the girl's dead body as if they had eyes of their own and were examining her, then she brought them back to her face again and, all the while, they continued to shake uncontrollably lost somewhere in a limbo between her dead son and her daughter's lifeless body.

That's when the mother let loose of all her emotions. Screaming her name, she grabbed hold of the girl's frail shoulders and shook her violently many times to try to revive her. Then, without warning, she let go of her tiny shoulders. The girl's head dropped and her skull cracked hard onto the decking. A wave of shock pulsed through those watching. Once again, the mother pressed her hands into her face and through the whole scene she repeated, "No," until the word sounded more like a mantra than a command.

Euly reached up after swallowing her last gulp of tea and touched her fingertips to her lips, not so much to dab any liquid off but instead to quiet the sad memory. She remembered how the man, whom she could barely visualize, clung to the edge of the pool inside the water next to the grief-stricken mother and watched.

Euly recalled police leading onlookers away and paramedics funneling past them toward the pool. That was the last time she remembered ever seeing the girl's parents. She didn't recall going to the funeral and resolved that she must not have.

Then, at some indeterminate point, the whole event disappeared from conversations. No one spoke about it and after a while they did something only survivors do — they let the memory die.

CHAPTER FIVE

Recently, Euly was opening up old wounds, purging, as psychologists call it. She realized that maybe Belle was doing a bit of purging herself when, yesterday, she disclosed to Euly one of her deepest secrets.

When she swallowed, Euly detected a hint of toothpaste mixed with Earl Grey. She murmured for Raz, in a half-hearted, irritated manner to, finally, take her spot. Her irritation, she reconciled, wasn't at all caused by the cat. Euly rolled her eyes when she thought about her day's duty – the real cause of irritation she'd impatiently directed onto her feline companion. The cause of her malaise was she would once again have to face her mother at the hospice and do so in the glaring light of this new information.

Euly's visits to see her mother had been daily for the past five months since the doctor cautioned that time was closing in on Belle. The doctors had said less than six months' time.

Thinking back on the few days before Belle took residence at Madrona Gardens, Euly and she made appointments to spend their few final days close together. They went through the contents of Belle's house wheedling through items to toss and those to keep, boxing some things and finding new homes for others –

her clothing and shoes, some dishes, some linens and furniture — some to stay with Euly, some to go with Enaya but everything in time would disappear. Belle's artwork was crated and found temporary solace in the loft. After winnowing down into two piles — one of papers to keep and one to recycle — all of Belle's important documents came to rest in the loft too. Her important documents went up and an assortment of sentimental cards and an old broken down journal one Euly had read many times always passing over a chunk of pages that had been torn out.

Euly thought about how she and her mother had had such fun talking, laughing, and genuinely enjoying the time they spent together. At the hospice as well, up until yesterday, Euly's visits had been out of true concern and love for Belle but, after her mother's admission, she guessed today's visit would feel strained.

Enaya wouldn't come up until the very end, she'd said. Her sister still lived in Phoenix. The truth was Enaya enjoyed the distance from her mother. Although she apologized to Euly about the situation, inside Euly knew Enaya was relieved, relieved from any responsibility of their mother and her failing health and Euly allowed it by reluctantly forgiving her sister.

Still, with their mother's advanced emphysema rattling loosely in her chest, the hacking and a constant bringing up of phlegm, was good enough reason for anyone to want to stay away. Euly hated to see her like this, this woman who had been so vibrant and alive not so long ago. Her mother, now this feeble woman in a hospice, was in vivid contrast to the person she used to be. At seventy-five, Belle had the weathered face of a well- reared lady, thin slumped shoulders, with blue highlights in her hair that women of her age rave about. Belle only wore worsted woolen skirts, pressed blouses, and her finest silk scarves. She loved her scarves, especially the periwinkle one, a scarf with a seam crosswise through it where it had once been cut or torn or, she couldn't exactly remember the reason.

When Belle did venture outside (and it was rare these days), she'd always wear a beret and her scarf. Belle said they made her look dapper, she said they made her look like an artiste.

Belle had shrunk in size and it was amusing for Euly to think how she now stood two inches taller than her own mother. Belle looked like a porcelain doll in a wheelchair. The wheelchair, a recent development, made it easier for Belle to get around. Her destroyed lungs made walking impossible for her. She said walking gave her the sensation similar to running top speed up a flight of stairs for any healthy person. She equated the feeling, the loss of breath, like having a wet towel over her face and trying to breathe through it.

Surprisingly to Euly, she'd welcomed the wheelchair. Euly felt her gut wrench knowing Belle wouldn't be around much past holidays, if that long.

The hospice, boasted amenities of finer hotels with a spa and beauty salon, and a staff made up of nurses and doctors. Madrona Gardens, set on twenty acres of verdant sloping hills in the heart of the island looked like a park with walkways and paths cut through beds of roses, hyacinth, and hydrangeas all mixed in with azaleas and tubers that appeared at the start of each season, like clockwork. The hospice even had a vegetable garden for its family members to tend if they desired. There, they called the patients 'family members' to make them feel at home during their stays. But, the ding of monitors, the reek of antiseptic, and the slap of shoes on tile floors as nurses sped to another dying patient's side, resonated so profoundly that it left you feeling only sadness with the whole thing. In Belle's case, it was a sadness that could have well been avoided. Belle's emphysema was caused by her cigarette smoking.

As a girl, Euly used to hide away in her room where she'd open windows to let the fresh desert air blow in, away from the smoke that hung in a thin cloud through the rest of the house. The putrid resin of smoke clung to drapery, furniture, and carpeting. It made their beautiful home where Euly was raised, seem ugly. Her parents smoked cigarettes at the breakfast table and at dinner, while watching TV or cleaning. It was if an unwanted house guest lived with them year long. Like some insane cousin the girls were forced to entertain and whom Euly wanted to lock away in a dungeon. Instead, their parents allowed him to roam freely and tag along with the girls.

Her anger flared again when she thought how Belle refused to give up the cigarettes even after they'd killed-off her father.

Don't cry. Don't cry.

Euly desperately didn't want to see her mother today looking like she'd been crying. She had to be strong. Then she resolved, maybe her mother's smoking was one thing her parent's had in common with each other, their one connection, after they'd divorced. They never stopped visiting each other and even spent holidays and birthdays together afterward. It was a relationship Euly didn't understand.

She got angry just then and wished she was more like her detached sister. Belle and Enaya had never been close. Increasingly through the years, however, when Euly and her sister talked, Enaya opened up. And, lately, her sister complained about their mother's manipulation with her. They'd had a fight the last time Enaya visited but neither of them would talk to Euly about it. Euly knew Enaya would certainly not put up with mother's newest revelation. Then, she wondered if Enaya might already know about this thing Belle had kept secret from them all these years. As it was on more than one occasion, Belle had sworn the girls to silence, together and separately. This matter was ripe for confidence.

But, she slipped up yesterday. When Belle saw a change in Euly's posture, she tried to recover by dissembling the information of her accidental unveiling by backtracking over crucial details. Her mother's recollection of the past undermined everyone else's. As she'd done to her so many times before, Belle set Euly into a tailspin. This one singularly important chapter in their family's life was now put up to question.

CHAPTER SIX

Euly fumed about it and knew one thing if nothing else about herself. She knew if she never had to visit her mother again, it would be okay.

After the thought rose and sunk, she felt pangs of shame hit her squarely in the stomach and she barely heard the curse escape from her lips as quickly as the thought entered her mind, the word escaped from her mouth. Euly's hand stopped mid-stroke through her cat's fur. Raz made a soft groan for her to continue.

"Sorry, Raz," she said and smoothed out her cat's coat. It also seemed to help her smooth out her mind from the sacrilegious thought.

What was it she'd just broken, the third or fourth commandment? If what Belle had said yesterday was true, her version of the past could make a mockery of her life, everyone's life in the small family. Even forty years later after her parent's divorce, so much life had been lived, but this one thing would make a farce of it all.

The information struck Euly hard on the back.

Euly wanted, no, wait... she *demanded* clarification.

And, it was at that precise second she vowed to set off on a fact-finding mission. She'd begin with her mother. She'd give Belle the opportunity to explain yesterday's comment and if her mother balked, she would do something else, anything else to get down to the truth.

Somehow, she would covertly ask her sister. She could go back to Phoenix and talk to Aunt Moon, anyone who might have information. What was more was, she could use the information she gathered for her memoir as well, it was a two-fold quest.

Euly rolled her eyes when she remembered how her mother had acted after she'd made the remark. Belle had turned the slip into a drama that slid from truth to excuse. This parsing out of reality from parody was something Euly was accustomed to doing with her mother. She didn't know when it happened but she had learned to stand on shaky ground during conversations with Belle.

CHAPTER SEVEN

They were flipping through some old photos together.

Lately, when Euly visited, Belle would drag out old memorabilia and divvy it up between things that would stay with her and things that would go to her sister.

Yesterday, her mother had given Euly a tattered photo album full of old black and white pictures, one Euly and her sister had grown accustom to seeing often as children. The photos, creased and worn, were trimmed as though the developer had used pinking shears around the edges.

Euly came upon a page with a photo of a group shot. It was of a backyard scene at the house where she'd grown. It was one of many neighborhood barbecue scenes.

The adults held up beers and cocktails while kids mulled around in front of a freshly-dug hole where a large empty metal pool sat in the background. Moxie, the family's shaggy black mutt, clung next to Belle's heel.

Belle looked stiff and wasn't smiling. She stood off to the side of Clive almost entirely out of the frame who stood with Sandy on the other side of Clive. Clive held up a can of Schlitz and looked like he was toasting the camera man.

Euly figured the photographer was her dad from his absence in the scene itself. Sandy's eyes were pointed downward but it also looked like the photo had been snapped at the exact time she'd decided to say something because her lips were partially opened.

Aunt Moon and Uncle Teddy flanked the other side of the photo with Uncle Teddy at the outermost edge leaning in and smiling wide.

Everyone's arms chained around each other's waists except for Belle's. Her arms were crossed in front of her stomach. In the center of the snapshot was a splotch that looked like someone had spilled coffee on the picture.

Euly handed the photo to Belle who pulled her readers up from the length of silver rope around her neck to examine the picture and she froze.

"I hate that picture." She held up the photo pinched between two fingers as if she would tear it.

"No! Mother! I want all the photos I can get of you." She sat forward quickly and snatched it from her grip. Its edge tore. "I can tape it." Euly could see Belle's face cramp in anger and knew if her mother could have fought her for the picture she would have.

"I hate that photo. Give it back now."

"Mother, no." Euly looked at her mother with an expression of hurt and confusion.

"I'm tired of this. I need to sleep." Belle coughed. It seemed like this one would be a bad attack but she held it off when she turned her head to the room's window. Her chest went through a rippling of small convulsions but Belle staved off the coughing fit. Euly noticed her mother wasn't actually looking outside but merely staring in the window's direction.

"Sorry, mother. I'll leave but I'm taking this with me." Euly placed the photo inside the album and held it up as she spoke.

"She ruined my life." She glared back at Euly. Her chin quivered but Euly stopped her by trying to be funny.

"I know, mother, I know. I'll cut her out of each picture. I promise. What do you think about that?"

"You can never cut her out." She believed she knew what her mother meant.

"Belle," Euly's tone turned parental. "Don't you think it's about time you got over dad's indiscretion?" She rolled her eyes at Belle. "You are divorced, you know? Plus, dad's been dead for twenty years." Euly's sarcastic manner irked Belle and she caught a word deep in her throat before letting her daughter have it — the truth she'd been hiding all along.

But, then, Belle let it dislodge with venom.

CHAPTER EIGHT

The second Belle let out her words, Euly's own well-practiced façade faltered.

Euly sat stunned and couldn't speak for an awkward few seconds but, in that time, Belle stared her daughter down. Euly's anger bubbled-up fast then dissipated just as fast when she decided to turn her attention toward her lap.

Belle had been persistent in her practice to sully the girls' memory of their father. Because of it, Euly had somehow taken up on his side, made her father her cause and justified his actions, if not openly to Belle then in the way she spoke to her.

As her mind whirled around her mother's brazen announcement, Euly focused her eyes downward. She replayed her mother's words. Still, even the second after saying them, Euly worried that maybe she'd gotten it wrong. Maybe she misunderstood.

She pressed her hands flat onto her legs and focused on them, a little trick she'd learned in order to keep her fingernails out of her mouth. Then, she put her hands together again and crossed each finger finally making the first two into a steeple.

As she fidgeted with her hands she noticed two of her knuckles were scraped. She used the time scrutinizing her fingers in an attempt to divert her eyes away from her mother's gaze.

Finally, Euly fumbled around for words then struck up some lame small-talk with Belle and did what she'd grown accustomed to doing – she found an excuse to leave. This time she lied and blamed her need to leave on a telephone call she expected from her publisher. Yesterday, the lie seemed to flow out easily like honey off its comb but today it stuck in her mind like a stinger.

Belle's leak of truth (and then the suppression of it) was buffered with excuses and two-steps, a normal trait for Belle who often down-played her own distasteful comments and actions, with rationalizations.

Euly wondered about the trait, if she'd at all inherited it or learned it. Of course, she knew the answer. She'd seen the method deployed so often as a child and as a young adult, of course she picked it up, like a gun out of its holster, ready for battle.

Now, the events that surrounded her parent's break-up so long ago began to ring out of control for Euly. Things she'd long forgotten heaved back up to the surface.

Left alone, the memories had scabbed over, under a gauze, lost somewhere between fact and fiction. Now, with Belle's confession--a ploy meant to elicit some distorted sense of forgiveness--Euly felt duped.

The only true person able to offer Belle forgiveness had long since died, her father, but he died ten years after they split. Yet, Belle unloaded this new story onto Euly quite expecting her to take the role she normally did, the role of the consoling daughter.

Belle expected Euly's forgiveness. And, in the last few weeks of Belle's life, Euly wondered if she was up to the task.

CHAPTER NINE

The tinny buzz whirring from the hospital TV gave a surreal, a fake quality to the seven-year-long war as the Iraqi correspondent explained the circumstances surrounding the latest suicide bombing attack.

"Why must you dwell on the past?" Belle turned her head back to the photo album, the one she intended to bestow on Euly.

"Me? Me dwell on the past? You're the one passing on photo albums." Euly shook her head and stopped talking. She was afraid she might say something she'd regret later. One of the nurses hurried past the door, the one with the squeaky shoes. They sounded just as though a person were chewing on rubber bands.

"We're looking at photos, is all. Can't you just enjoy that?" Belle returned her attention to another photo. Her nurse walked in with a pitcher of water and two glasses. Euly noticed a fresh aura follow her as though she'd bathed in lavender soap. Her makeup was slight but set off her exotic features even more, her red pouting lips and deer eyes. Her white uniform contrasted her dark skin, as dark as an Ethiopian, Euly thought.

Belle lifted her head as an acknowledgement and then looked back down at the album. The nurse's nametag read, Artis.

"Look, dear, here's one of you and Enaya in your ballet clothes. You both were so sweet when you danced." Artis came around to Belle's side and looked at the photo. She smiled at Belle and nudged her with the back of her hand. Then, she looked up at Euly and smiled at her.

Before Artis left she began humming a pining gospel tune. Euly listened as the song faded down the hall. She strained when it became nothing more than a whistle in her ear.

She took the photo from her mother. Euly, at age six, was wearing pink tights and pink leotards her arms were high above her head, her smile was wide and her eyes were closed but her lips were pressed together and she posed in first position.

With her eyes closed the way they were you got the feeling the sun was aimed straight into her faces. Her sister, clad in black, made a scrunched face protecting her eyes from the glare. Euly flipped the photo over. In her mother's hand she'd written 7/4/1963.

Euly felt at a loss what to do next. Her mother obviously was not going to bring up yesterday's topic without prodding.

"Mother."

"Yes, dear." Belle looked at her daughter. Euly could see the muscle in her mother's jaw tighten when she clenched her teeth, as if she was preparing herself for a punch.

"About yesterday."

"What about yesterday? See, can't you just let things go?" She squinted her remark in a dare.

"Mother, this isn't about me."

"Well, then, perhaps it's none of your business."

Euly felt her demeanor crumble.

Over the intercom, a woman's voice called out in a subdued plea for Doctor Hamlin to come to guest room 17. Belle, the resident of guest room 11, would not go lightly into yesterdays' subject, a subject Euly needed to clarify, to understand.

"If it's about the family, then I suppose it is my business."

"My, don't you have a high opinion of yourself. Not every little detail about our lives is something subject to your understanding, Euly."

"No? Well, you brought it up and I suppose since you did, you might want to explain yourself."

"And if I don't?"

"If you don't? What the hell do you mean by that, mother?"

"Euly, my past, our past isn't something everyone needs to know about nor do I care to explain. Except it or not. Either way, it's not my problem."

"You brought it up!" Euly's voice echoed off the window and bounced back at both women. They could hear the rustle of usual noises in the hall of the building die down.

"Try to keep your voice down. Seriously, Euly, show some decorum."

"Fine. Fine." Euly searched for something to say but was angry and frustrated by her mother's retreat and refusal to speak. She picked up her purse and found a tissue and wiped the oil from her nose when she folded the tissue back into her purse she found a packet of gum.

"Gum?"

Her mother nodded.

Euly handed Belle a stick of gum. Belle took off the gum's wrapper and Euly offered her hand to take it and throw it away. They both sat quietly and chewed. With her hands on the photo album, Belle watched Euly who was still fumbling and zipping up a compartment inside her purse. After she was done she latched the purse and set it next to the chair beside her. She looked at her mother and sighed.

"You know, mother. Micaiah was like a brother to me."

"I won't do this, Euly." Belle looked away and out the window.

"When he died, I was crushed. Do you remember?"

"Of course I remember. He was only fourteen. How can I not remember." Belle frowned at Euly.

"It was awful."

Belle's chin began to quiver and she anxiously searched the tray for something to wipe her nose. Euly pulled out more tissue and handed it to her mother.

"Why are you doing this to me? Can't you leave it alone? I won't talk about it. Not with you or anyone else! Drop it, Euly."

"This is so unfair, mother. You drop this bomb and then tell me you won't talk about it?" She gave her mother a moment to respond. "Mother if Micaiah was my brother," Belle rolled her eyes away, "then I have every right to know about it!" Once again, Euly's voice arced. But, before Belle could reprimand her, Euly spoke.

"Don't tell me to keep my voice down. I'm an adult now. Are you going to explain about Micaiah, or not?"

Belle looked stiff and lifted her chin. "Not."

"Then, I'll have to find out on my own, I guess."

"Euly, no."

"I decided last night that if you weren't truthful with me today, I'd just have to take matters into my own hands."

"Euly..."

"I'm leaving for Phoenix on Friday. You have two days to think about it, to come clean."

As she spoke, Euly picked up her purse and stood. "I'm fifty, mother. Do you think that's old enough to deal with the truth?"

"Do you think I'm old enough to deal with the truth." Belle always had a way of pulling rank on Euly.

But, Euly had enough.

"Don't correct me, mother. We're not in school." Euly walked to the door but stopped. "So, what is it? Shall I stay?"

Her mother opened her mouth to speak but stopped short, then turned her head casually back to the photos and began flipping through them.

"God, mother, you're infuriating!" She grumbled and walked out.

CHAPTER TEN

The sizzling garlic pattered like one million army ants tramping across a forest floor and echoed through the kitchen drifting lightly into the den where Geoff watched golf on the television.

Euly's mind replayed the conversation with her mother as she chopped with a heavy chef's knife. She conducted a silent quarrel with herself under her breath after quartering an onion and slicing it into halves, and cubing those crosswise into inch-sized pieces. She then began cutting the smaller pieces into even smaller pieces until she'd diced the onion. As she continued to cut in fast hard strokes, chopping the onion into a mince, its peppery fumes hit her in the nose and her tear ducts and sinuses let loose.

She tried to wipe her eyes on her sleeve near her shoulder and sniffed loudly but continued to chop through it all. As her speed quickened in a race to finish, she nicked her finger with the knife's sharp blade.

She grumbled out. "Dammit!" And dropped the knife onto the counter, flipped on the faucet, and grabbed a paper towel to hold to her wounded finger.

"Are you okay, honey?" Geoff asked without turning his head from the TV.

"I cut myself."

"Again?"

"Don't." Euly wasn't joking but Geoff couldn't tell. His attention was split between Tiger Woods and her. Euly heard Geoff giggle under the drone of a gallery clapping softly and commentators as they gave a blow-by-blow in their typical mundane hushed voice. Euly wasn't amused and headed past him to the laundry room where they kept a first-aid kit.

"Again, get it?" Euly walked by ignoring Geoff. "Are you okay?"

Euly refused to answer him and thrashed about through the room slamming cupboard doors and setting the kit noisily onto the counter.

"I asked... are... you... okay?"

Euly came out with a bandage on her finger and bruised feelings.

"Why do you want to know? All you do is sit there on your butt, watch TV, and eat."

"Here we go."

"Here we go?" Euly nearly gagged trying to keep from saying what she wanted to say. "Forget it. Your dinner will be ready soon." She stomped back into the kitchen. She wondered if Geoff felt her anger scudding through the airwaves.

"You know, honey, that's not all I care about. I love," he paused and then continued to tease her, "I love Jonathan." His tricks wouldn't work on her tonight, even when it involved the dog. His voice was happy but Euly wasn't in the mood for happy.

"You know what Geoff?" She stalled before saying what she wanted, to insult him, to hurt him, instead she said what was really on her mind, "I'm leaving."

"Geez, Euly. I'm only kidding." He turned around and stared limp-faced.

"Well, I'm not." Geoff rose from the couch. "I need to get away. I'm leaving for Phoenix this Friday."

"What? Good God, Euly. Where did this come from?"

She turned back to her cooking and scraped the onion into the sauté mixture with her knife. As she wiped her hands on her apron, Geoff came over and sat at the bar.

"Talk to me. What's going on?"

"Nothing, and that's exactly why I have to leave."

"What are you talking about? How much is this going to cost us?"

"Christ, Geoff. I'm making money too, remember?" She shook her head and turned away from him, pulled the stems off of three tomatoes and rinsed them trying to avoid water hitting her bandage. "Anyway, your stores make great money. God, Geoff! We have a retirement fund that's ready to split at the seams and I can't take a little time to myself? Why do I always have to justify leaving and you just do whatever the hell you want. Go on golf trips, ski trips, all that shit's okay, but me I have to leave and you give me the third-degree. Why the double-standard?"

"Why do you have to go?" His attention was diverted away from golf and entirely on his wife. "What?"

"You said you have to go, why?"

"I just do. I have to get away."

"From me?"

"Why does everything have to be about you?" She jutted out her chin daring him to answer.

"Well is it about me? Do I have something to worry about?"

"It's not about you. It's about me."

"Okay, so what about you is this about?"

"Good grief. That is the worst sentence."

"Come on. You know what I mean." She refused to engage him further. Euly paused and looked down at the tomatoes she'd been slicing. The sloppy juice ran everywhere and was spilling into the ruts of the cutting board. They were too ripe to put into a salad so she slipped them into the sauté along with the garlic and onions. Within seconds she decided they'd have a red sauce over some pasta, angel hair. The garlic and onion weakened under the heat with an added transparent quality letting her know it was time to season, add the tomatoes and red wine. After sprinkling coarse salt she ground in fresh pepper then stirred. She worked with her injured finger up and unavailable as she cubed more tomatoes for the sauce. Their perfume mesmerized her and she stole one cube and ate it. Its familiar sappy acid slid down her throat and nearly choked her. Grabbing the bottle of cabernet, she pulled the cork out by her teeth. The popping made her worry if she'd bruised the juice. She poured a glass for herself first then Geoff and then added some into the sauté pan. She stirred and watched the mixture bubble. As she worked, she seemed to go inside herself as she stirred. She acted as though she'd forgotten Geoff was even there.

"Euly? What's going on?" The softness in his voice made her take in a deep breath. She wondered if she'd been breathing at all. "Euly. You have to talk to me." He'd gone one fraction too far with the demand.

"I don't have to do anything of the sort. I'm leaving for a few days, maybe a week. You can go to see your family when you want to and I can see mine."

"You're leaving your mother?"

Euly turned to Geoff. She still held the knife and used it to emphasize her point. Geoff watched it as she conducted a silent symphony about her mother.

"My mother will be fine alone. She likes it that way. Anyway, don't try to make me feel guilty. I'm not guilty about her or leaving here or anything, okay? I have to go and I will. The end." She swung the knife back. She set it down with a thud against the counter and began tearing up thick leaves of romaine and dropped each bunch elegantly into the deep cherry colored salad bowl. Geoff watched silently. Peripherally, she could see he was still staring at her. Then, she slammed both hands onto the counter. "Dammit. I don't have to give you a reason."

"So, I'm just supposed to accept that you're leaving because you have to in this fit of anger. Is that right?"

"Yes."

"You can't hear the selfishness in that?" Euly faced him and walked directly to the opposite side of the bar across from him.

"Look, Geoff. You never seem to give me the opportunity to object to you running off and being with the guys whenever you feel like it. I'd appreciate the same treatment. If you don't mind."

"Well, I do mind, Euly. Are you seeing your ex?"

The thought nearly knocked her down. She hadn't thought of her ex-husband in years nor did she have any feelings for him. Then, the insult of the comment set in.

"Oh. Good grief. Of course, this must be about your manhood, right? Why else would I leave? No. I'm not going off to see the man whom I divorced nor am I having some illicit affair with anyone else. I'm going. I can't tell you why all I know is that I have to go. When I find what I'm looking for, you'll be the first to know. How's that?"

Their fight was escalating. She could feel it spinning out of control. She wanted a drink — a good stiff shot of scotch. She stood there leaning into the counter at her husband and stopped for fear the fight would wrangle them into something irreparable.

"I'm getting a drink. You want one?"

"Boy, do I." He breathed out heavily and she walked out of the kitchen through the closed set of French doors and into the dining room. The air felt crisp on her hot face. They closed off that room once the weather turned bad but all she wanted to do right now was to walk outside in the dark and cold of the frosty night. Alone.

She opened the liquor cabinet and felt a pang of guilt knife at her gut. She was resorting to an alcoholic beverage to calm her nerves, to make her feel better. She wondered about the old stigma of writers and drinking. While she poured two shots into the crystal glasses, she thought about the stereotypical alcoholic writers of the past, Hemingway, Poe — her heroes. She slammed her drink in a quick flip of the head backward then refilled her glass. Hemingway would be proud. She felt her mood lighten almost immediately.

When she returned with two glasses full, Geoff had turned his attention to golf again but remained on the stool where she'd left him.

"Here." She set his drink in front of him. "Want ice."

"Sure. Look, Euly, whatever it is you feel you need to do, do it. I won't ask any more questions. I love you. Do you understand me?"

Euly nodded that she did and raised her glass up for a silent toast. She sipped and went to the freezer for the ice. Geoff turned his attention back to the television.

"Honey, did you see that shot? Man-o-man, he's amazing. Did I tell you about the odds on Tiger?" After that, his voice faded out of her ears and her mind wandered. She stopped making dinner and took her drink into the living room where there was no TV, no talk of golf, no husband just quiet, she longed for quiet. Outside, a rustling wind from fall exiting and winter making its entrance thumped against the window panes. The final call of birds in the early evening meant the season was leaving. She left the lights off and walked soberly to their leather sofa, the sofa she had bought on a whim for Geoff because she imagined them lying naked on it making love but they never did and she wondered if, after six years of marriage, they ever would.

*   *   *

"Jill make sure everyone knows I'll be unavailable for a couple of weeks, maybe longer. I have to go, you know." Euly's voice, filled with trepidation, rung palpable.

Euly knew her assistant would make sure to tell everyone at the paper that Euly would be unavailable. She bid her to have fun and good luck as if going to a Club Med, as if luck was a good thing.

Geoff yelled to her where he stood by the door on the first floor for her hurry and something about missing the plane and visiting her mother too. Euly shook her head and ended the phone conversation. After she hung up she worried if she might have a job when she got back. Writing jobs were few and far between. It was a

Russia of economies for writers. There were writers standing in line for work. Writing obituaries wasn't glamorous but at least she made money from them, and she needed her money, her independence.

"I'll be right there."

"You're not going to have a lot of time with your mother if we don't leave soon."

Geoff had a habit of rushing Euly that simply infuriated her.

"Two minutes isn't going to make or break our visit." She'd neglected to tell Geoff about the heated conversation with her mother the day before.

"I'll go start the car."

Euly ran into the bathroom. She needed to empty her bladder one more time before they left the house, she needed to put on lipstick, and more than anything she needed to take two aspirin. She raced from the toilet zipping her pants and stretching out her neck by tipping it far left then right again. She rubbed the muscles on top of her shoulders and ran cold water. The muscles refused to loosen and she decided rubbing her jaw muscle might work better, but she had no time for it and gave up the notion, opened the medicine cabinet, popped two pills and stuck her hand under the faucet where she pooled water in her palm to drink. After dabbing her mouth, she found her lipstick, slicked it over her lips, and stuck it into her right pant pocket.

She was ready. She raced down the stairs, threw on the coat, the one Geoff had hung out on the end of the banister for her and walked out of the house. As she lifted her leg into Geoff's truck, she was still organizing her thoughts. "Did you get my bag?"

"It's in the back."

"My purse too?"

"*Everything* in the back."

She closed the door and latched her seat belt and Geoff cruised down the circular drive toward its end.

"Wait!" Euly screamed. Geoff rolled his eyes and depressed the brakes.

"What did you forget?"

"Stay here. I'll be back in a sec." She unlatched her seat belt and jumped out of the truck. She left the door open to make getting back in easier for her.

CHAPTER ELEVEN

At her desk, she found the recorder. She stuffed it into her coat pocket and walked over to Jonathan who was lying on the back of the couch watching her. She patted his back and kissed his forehead.

"Mommy will be back soon." She raced back out to where she'd left Geoff idling. The radio newsman talked about Bush sending more troops into Basra.

"That was rude."

"What was rude? I forgot something." Euly didn't like the way he tried to get her to respond to his off-hand remark. She rolled her eyes when she turned to re-latch the seatbelt.

"Leaving the door open. It's cold, you know."

"Sorry." She spoke quietly and quickly.

"What did you forget?" He put the car back into gear and pulled to the end of the drive.

"I wanted to say goodbye to Jonathan." She looked out the window.

"You left me in the cold to say goodbye to the dog?"

"Sorry." She wouldn't speak anymore, she resolved to herself. It was better they didn't talk when Geoff was in a mood.

"We'll be lucky if we can see your mother for five minutes." His comments added to the tightening sensation she felt in her throat and she pinched two fingers behind her head and began to massage as they drove away from the house.

CHAPTER TWELVE

"Geoff? Will you be a dear and get us all some coffee from the cafeteria?"

"Sure Belle but we have to leave shortly." He raised his eyebrows and stared strongly at Euly.

She turned to her mother who was staring at her.

"I wish you wouldn't go."

"That makes two of you."

"What do you want from me, Euly. Haven't I been a good mother?" Euly bit at her thumbnail. "Get your fingers out of your mouth. You're not twelve." Belle sighed and folded her arms over her chest with disapproval. She was wearing her pajamas still not normal for her mother who always made sure she was 'up and at 'em' before the break of dawn. It was nearly ten in the morning.

"Aren't you feeling well this morning, mother?"

"I feel fine. Why should you care about my feelings." Belle had a knack for changing the meanings of things.

"Mother. You still have a chance to come clean."

"I don't have to tell you anything. I don't have anything to come clean to."

Geoff reappeared with three machine-made coffees balancing in his hands. He placed Belle's on the nightstand and handed Euly hers then sipped at his burning his tongue.

"Kee-Rikey! These are always so freaking hot. I burned my fingers getting them here." Euly arose.

"Well, it's now or never, mother." Geoff looked at Euly then her mother.

Belle turned her head away.

"Euly, let's go, you'll miss your flight."

"Yes, I will. Goodbye mother."

Belle refused to look at her.

"Come on, honey. Let's leave your mother alone. Belle, she'll be back in a week or so. Right Euly?" He gave her a strained look. "But, I'll be over to see you."

Belle smiled at Geoff and nodded and when he walked to the door nearer to Euly, Belle glared at her daughter behind his back. Euly glared back.

CHAPTER THIRTEEN

Like most airports, SeaTac hummed with white noise. People talked on cell phones, a voice over the loudspeaker, children screaming, carts beeping, televisions broadcasters droning on about the latest news—the BP oil spill—and wheels rolling luggage along cold tile floor.

Euly felt disoriented by the rhythm, not at all like a kid jumping back onto a bike.

Back in the city, going back to any city, almost made her motion-sick from the sway of its rapid pace – a pace she'd long fought to get away from and found she was losing the battle every time she returned. It was borne in her, the stink of traffic and diesel from buses, the din of airplanes and no geese, like on the island. However, the city's robust pace made her feel alive again in an upside-down sort of way – dangling in its web.

She admitted, the trouble to simply get off the island had begun to wear her down. A bridge would help the situation but without one, people on the island were held captive unless they took a chartered a ferry or a plane.

Euly needed this break, the time away. She was fighting the urge to scream, an urge to leave making her want to scream. She fought these urges by getting away. Did that make sense? She wasn't sure but, for now, it was the only reason she could rely on, the here and the now of it.

One of the questions looked like a billboard.

The urge to leave what?

The question slipped over her head like a neon sign, flashing on and off, repeating. Geoff.

Did she love him? She wondered. She could honestly say she did but she still longed to be alone, independent, making her own choices, living a life she'd envisioned by herself – one she'd gotten a glimmer of right after her first divorce yet here she stood, in the thick of it, in another marriage.

She punched her eTicket information into the airline's monitor, retrieved her ticket and went to the counter. She hoisted her bag onto the metal scale.

"May I see some ID?"

Euly fumbled for the passport in her vest pocket and held it out for the ticketing agent.

"Just one bag?" After the overly made-up ticketing agent tagged her luggage handle she pulled the bag off the scale and onto a moving rubber runway behind her.

"Yes."

"Thank you, Ms. Winger. Gate C4. You'll begin boarding in forty-five minutes."

"Thank you."

Ticket agent. All they really were nowadays were luggage assistants, bellboys with better uniforms. It was the same as calling a server in cafeterias a waitress.

Her sharp metered steps struck loud against the composite tile of the airport floors as she walked to the security gates. She stood in line waiting with her shoes held by two fingers and her shoulder bag held closely against her chest. The line method moved and mimicked the same motion as an assembly line — grab the tray, set in the shoes, set in the jackets, set in purses — the forward movement was only broken when one woman had forgotten to combine all of her liquid items into a see-through bag. Since the war, it was a new development and level of security that had everyone baffled and yet everyone but this one woman remembered to do it.

No longer were no eye creams allowed in the passenger area for fear they'd be used to heist the plane in flight. The woman had to relinquish what Euly noticed were some spendy Estee Lauder emollients and creams, a set of high-priced shampoo and conditioner, and a bottle of perfume. The woman stepped out of line to discuss the matter with the man-in-charge, a Transportation Security

Agent, and the assembly line continued.

Hotdogs sizzled and glistened on a rotisserie as she walked past by a fast food deli. Their meaty juice sizzled and their scent waft through the air sending a pang into her stomach. She needed to eat before boarding. She resolved to by a pre-packaged sandwich, an iced tea and a bag of potato chips from the next vendor down from the hotdogs.

While she ate, she avoided eye contact with people sitting around her. A man appeared as though he was talking to himself but when he turned, she noticed his earphone. He looked ridiculous. He was making overstated gestures so people would notice him. He was trying to give an impression of importance by telling whomever was on the other line what they needed to do, how to do it and by what time. He sickened her. Geoff sickened her. Her mother sickened her. She stopped eating and put her hand to her mouth. She couldn't believe she just thought that about her mother and husband.

She was still trying to fold the information into her mind, trying to understand why her mother would keep from them all these years that Micaiah was their brother.

*   *   *

"I thought you'd be happy. You always said you wished you'd had a brother."

"Mother! What you're telling me is that Aunt Moon and dad had an affair and Micaiah is my half-brother. It's not what I meant when I said that I'd wished I had a brother. Good grief."

Her mother could unravel her with such ease.

She felt her heart palpitating. She'd had one panic attack in her life and it was more than she'd ever hoped for. She remembered the helpless feeling of not being able to breathe but, at the same time, that was all that she was doing. She couldn't stop her heart from racing, she felt dizzy.

Her mother was pushing her limits. Euly had been doing well since her mother's health started to fail. She'd assumed a more mature attitude about their relationship, the reckless barbs thrown by Belle were simply deflected by the understanding that her mother would soon be gone and she'd miss her. She knew she would. But, this new revelation was unconscionable. I thought you'd be happy. How dare she.

"Okay. Back up. What happened?"

"They had sex and she had a baby. It doesn't get more complicated than that."

"I mean, when? where? How did they get away with the secret all these years?"

"Why does that matter at this stage of the game? Anyway, poor Micaiah is dead now. I just thought you should know. You don't have to do anything about it. Just accept it for what it is."

"Why didn't you tell me when he died? Or before?"

"Drop it, Euly. It's old news."

"To you! Does Enaya know?"

"I doubt it."

"You doubt it or you know for a fact she doesn't?"

"I know for a fact."

Euly glared at her mother trying to determine if she was telling her the truth. Belle always told Enaya everything first like the time she decided she wanted to move to the island and build a place on Euly's property. Instead of discussing it with Euly first, she tossed the idea around with Enaya. It was when she finally asked Euly if she could make room for her did she mention Enaya. Enaya thinks this and Enaya says that. Euly remembered feeling that if she'd refused her mother it would have been an affront to both her mother and her sister.

"Quit glaring at me." Euly turned away.

"I have to go anyway. I have, uh, my publisher is supposed to call me.

"Fine."

"Do you need anything? I'm running by the store later and I can pick up whatever you want." She was fumbling again. She fidgeted. She grabbed her purse but then didn't commit and wiped the hair out of her face. Her hands finally fell onto her lap and she began to play nervously with her fingers.

"Don't do anything with this, Euly."

"I've gotta go. Love you mother." It sounded strained. She bent over and kissed her mother on the cheek.

CHAPTER FOURTEEN

She unclipped it and pulled it out of her notebook. A corner was creased and she knew it would fall off if she didn't tape it for strength. She regarded the photo with the utmost care. It seemed like a last-ditch effort to spur on the memory of the times for the people she would interview. After repairing it, she placed it tenderly into the journal and carried it in her purse.

Tomorrow she would meet up with Enaya. But for now she just wanted to lie down on the bed and rest.

She remembered everything there sitting alone in her hotel room. It was hot even for November. The desert air slowed down in the heat. The coolness of the island pulled on Euly's sleeve tugging her back. She felt homesick for the first time in many years. It was odd.

The last time she felt that way was when she was a girl. They'd all driven to the Petrified Forest – the place, the year, 1965 – the time was shortly after Pearl Harbor and a repercussion of that war and then the Korean War. They called Japanese soldiers during that time of anti-Japanese mentality, Japs and Nips. She'd heard her father say those words. He knew how it felt being a dark-skinned Arab. She didn't understand it and now four decades later she was seeing the bigotry shift over to her people the way it had to the Japanese back then.

She looked out at the hotel window. The lower desert differed from the high desert in climate. The high desert at least produced a thick cover of snow in January. Snow in the low desert was unusual at best. If it ever snowed it ended up highly-publicized with news cameras and reporters all gathered around a small corner where it fell and where neighbors built a dwarf snowman. In a place where the sun scorches at a rate of 122 Fahrenheit in July and August, snow rarely blessed Phoenix, even in the winter.

She remembered everything here.

CHAPTER FIFTEEN

The morning was sunny — nothing unusual for the desert. Back then, in the early morning before anyone thought of rising, the earth sang. She would lie in bed and let an orchestra of crickets and birds blanket her. It started slow as if one single cricket had cracked a baton on a podium and began its orchestra. It awakened and needed company. Tap, tap, tap.

And, slow like a drop of rain on parched soil that makes people look up to the heavens and bless the rain gods, there in the desert cricket legs chirped out in the high-pitch of a violin, only the way a violin or a cricket can perform their music. Crickets were harbingers of morning coming. And, the evenings popped were given up to dense clouds of white flies so thick you had to laugh close-mouthed for fear of sucking in gulps of them.

But, only four months there during the late, late fall, winter, and early-early spring it seemed like a cooler version of summer. The other seven months, were full-on heatstroke summer and from late March to early November felt more like hell. Summers weren't filled with butterflies, asters, and hydrangeas, people having barbecues, playing volleyball. They were filled with panting dogs, dying pigeons, and old people being rushed to emergency from exposure. The cooler time —

that four-month respite — proved the sole reason people left the east coast, the northwest, the Midwest, and the Gulf States to relocate. You could layout in swim suits in the winter! Something not many folks could do in the rest of the contiguous U.S. How they balanced it with the rest of the year, she could barely understand.

She could never forget childhood or those scents that transported her to other place in time — creosote burning under a single band of sun that never lets up and pasty school cafeteria pizza still on her tongue. School chums and she standing outside red brick walls of homeroom waiting for Mrs. Potts to return from her lunch break. Mrs. Potts in the fourth grade meant two things: she was nine years old and she loved homeroom class. For whatever reason, the girls standing around were discussing family heritages, probably from something they'd learned that day. One girl was of English stock, another Irish, and so on. When they asked Euly, she explained to them she was Lebanese. They howled. They said, "She's a lesbian, she's a lesbian!" Euly wondered now if they really knew what the word meant. But, the other girls jeered and poked fun at the similarity of the words. Euly vehemently and red-facedly corrected them by saying in broken and slow words so even they could get it, "Leb-a-nese." It wasn't funny and they didn't let up. When Mrs. Potts came back from lunch the taunting stopped. The girls scuffled and chatted back into the room – back to their seats. All was forgotten, for them, but for Euly the burn of their barbs stuck under her skin and lingered.

After that, she and Enaya were different. They stood apart from the other girls with creamy milk-fed skin who ate mashed potatoes and gravy. It was at that young age she remembered feeling strange. For Euly it was like having a noose around her neck.

The teasing followed her into high school and she hated it there too. She wanted to fast-forward life into college where she thought people might be different, smarter, involved with learning and not only concerned about being popular. But, why she hadn't told the others girls her heritage was her mother's, from her mother's side of the genetic stitch, she hadn't a clue. Belle was a mix of English, Irish and Dutch. And, because of the mix in gene pools, they didn't look different, aside from a fewer poisonous reminders from her slip in elementary school, they were no worse for the wear.

In college, there was a wild mix of ethnicities shapes and colors and Euly no longer stood out as odd. Plus, when she did reveal her background, people didn't seem to care or, at least, it wasn't profound like it was when she and her friends were seven. Anyway, those days it was the blacks and Jews getting the brunt of bigotry, they were the ones collectively treated as second-class citizens, not people like Euly and Enaya, not then. Sometimes honesty didn't pay. The memories flooded back as she watched the sun closing out another day.

CHAPTER SIXTEEN

She looked older. Euly detected the finest lines around Enaya's sea green eyes but she still looked good. She wondered why someone with the color of her eyes didn't live near the ocean the way Euly did. Backwards, she thought. Enaya, the one with ocean-eyes, living in the desert and Euly, with her brown eyes, living on an island. It was backwards. Euly pulled at her sleeve when she noticed wrinkles set in at her shirt's elbows. She compared how Enaya was ordered, the proper way she sat in her chair, her beige linen suit looking fresh, her short cropped hair thick and pulled perfectly behind her ears and, her earlobes, studded with what looked to be two-carat diamonds in each. "Jimmy."

Euly's attention was distracted and she looked into her sister's eyes. "Hmm?"

"Jimmy, he got them for me." She flicked at one of her lobes. She'd seen her looking at the earrings. Euly angled her eyes down to the table. "Said they put him back a pretty penny." There it was, the expected jab to let Euly know in one of her many ways how much money they made.

"Well, they're lovely."

Right away, Euly felt uncomfortable. She didn't have clothes for the desert anymore. She wore a long-sleeved jersey top and jeans. Her boots looked urbane but were more suited for Seattle than Phoenix. She had a tight silk scarf around her neck that began to get hot, even hotter, so she untied it and let it hang loosely on her shoulders. She was tired from traveling. The waiter came back to the table expecting them to order.

"I'll have the Pinot Gris." Enaya folded her menu and handed it to the waiter making sure not to make eye contact with him. Euly couldn't help but feel a pang of disgust.

"I'll have the Cab, thank you." She smiled directly at the man and he thanked them both for the order with a tip of his head, first at Euly then at her sister.

"You're on a fact-finding mission, are you?" Enaya sipped her water then dabbed the corners of her mouth.

"Yeah. Yes." Euly folded and re-folded her napkin.

"What facts are you trying to scare up?"

She looked at Enaya. Her older face was no less critical. Squinting her eyes the way she did when she didn't believe something you said, added to her age. A busboy came with a silver pitcher to fill their drinks. Euly whispered thanks to him and grabbed the glass not so much because she was thirsty but to still her thoughts before speaking to Enaya. She wanted to tell her what a bitch she thought she was – how she'd always been an uppity bitch – but Euly took a sip instead.

"Things about our past." She dug into her bag and brought out the journal and set it next to her plate.

"Things..."

"Yes, things about our family. What really happened."

Euly sensed her sister's skepticism grow by the look on her face. Enaya shook her head.

"You're funny. Always trying to make something out of nothing."

"You think mother and dad's divorce is nothing?"

It never failed. Whenever they got together, they got to the meat of it.

"Nothing? No. I wouldn't say that, Eu." Euly bristled at the way her sister shortened her name. She was testing her patience. "Not nothing but not something either."

"Wow, Enaya. You really have a talent for words." Now, she dug in. Enaya had always been jealous that Euly had become a professional writer, that she was making a living of it. But, Enaya handled herself well.

"So! It's nice we've gotten all of that out of the way." She smiled because of their little battle. "Really, Euly, it's good to see you. I miss you, you know?"

"No. I didn't Enaya. You don't call all that often so, no, I don't know. Your distance speaks volumes."

"Jealous?"

Euly laughed. Her sister had the knack for not assuming the responsibilities others would. She supposed Enaya had good reason. With a family and a career she had a well-stacked plate.

"Maybe but just a little."

"Really. What are you doing here, Euly?"

"I was visiting with mother the other night. She's getting a little weepy and forgiving these days but still has a kick, you know." She opened the journal. The waiter brought their wine glasses and placed them on the table.

"Just a sec." Enaya ordered. She tasted the wine he'd set in front of her. She nodded and he walked away. "She always gets that way when she knows she's wrong... or she's dying, I suppose."

"Crap, Enaya. Can you at least try to appear sad mother is dying. For me?"

"Sorry, dear. I forget that mother's favorite is so sensitive these days."

"Good God, Enaya. Do you always have to be such a raving bitch?"

"And you're the writer."

"Don't try to intimidate me. I've earned the title from years of hard work." She hated how she always ended up defending herself. "You know what? I'm not so hungry after all. Why don't you go home to your tidy little house and family and read another book. While you're doing that I'll be living, exploring, going on another treasure hunt." She took a long slug of her wine and set it down, eyeing her over the glass. She knew the treasure hunt comment would bite deep. She wiped her mouth removing all her lipstick and pushed out her chair.

"Very nice. Nice drama, nice punch at the end. You shouldn't have given up acting. Really, Eu, you have talent."

"Screw off." She started to leave, and then stopped. She turned and walked back. "First off, this is my hotel. You can leave."

"This is my city. You can leave." Enaya enjoyed riling her sister and she let off a smirk.

"I was born here, Enaya. You were born in some cow town in the Midwest. You can leave."

"Bravo. Now, see? I'm right. You would've made a fine actor. I'm always right. I'm your older
sister."

"That makes you always older not always right."

Euly sat down again. "You leave."

"No."

"Then, tell me what you remember, you hag of a sister." They were on speaking terms again and it felt homey, like they were kids fighting.

"Remember what, brat."

"About mother and dad. The divorce. Everything. Creep."

"Everything could take hours. Fat head."

"I'm not leaving until I find out so I guess I have hours."

"I don't."

"You have until midnight when you turn into a snake again." Euly glared out a smile.

"I missed you."

Euly smiled but each knew they weren't finished. A silly argument had not been settled in the four years since she'd seen her sister. Four years since their grandmother's death. Things didn't go as well as they might've with her sister then as Euly recalled. They'd had a stupid fight about who'd get their grandmother's china. Enaya won when their mother stepped in to decide.

"How's my china?"

"It's stunning."

Euly smirked and settled back into her chair. She re-folded the napkin on her lap, grabbed her glass and drank from it, set it back down and looked at her sister. She pulled out the photo and slid it over to Enaya on the smooth surface of the linen. "Do you remember what led up to the divorce?"

"Yours or mother's?"

"Come on. I'm serious."

Enaya was taking her time giving Euly anything. She'd always been like that. She flicked her eyebrows and shrugged. She picked up the photo and squinted for focus, for effect.

"That's an old one. Where'd you get it?"

"Mother. She's going through all of her photo albums, one by one, and splitting them up between us."

"That's fair."

Euly neglected to mention her pile was greater and switched the subject. "Hey, do you remember that little girl who drowned?"

"What little girl who drowned?"

"You remember. At the Maharajan."

Enaya's eyes opened in recognition.

"Oh yeah. Wasn't that awful?"

"I remember it in stops and starts. Pieces, you know? I think I've filled in a lot that may not be right but, then, maybe not. I don't know."

They stopped talking and both seemed to fade into the vision. "I've been thinking about it a lot lately. I don't know why."

"Death." She examined the photo more closely as she spoke then handed it back to Euly.

"Yeah."

"No. I mean you're thinking about death a lot."

"I suppose."

"Well, you're living with it aren't you. You visit her daily, right?"

"Mother? Yes. I see her every day."

"Don't you think that's why you're here really, to get away?"

"No. No, I'm here because I want to find out what really happened between them. Why they Geoff."

Enaya lifted her eyebrows. "I didn't say anything about Geoff." Euly looked at her lap and played with her napkin but she didn't broach the subject. "Look, Eu, they split. Why drum it up again? They were miserable together, remember? They fought all the time."

"Do you remember that photo?"

"Not really. I was like, what, twelve?"

"Yeah, ten, eleven, twelve, something like that. Oh, and not always."

"Not always, what?"

"They didn't always fight."

"Yes, they did. Always."

"Not when we were little. Not when that little girl drowned. They didn't fight then. It was later when we were teenagers, remember?"

"Maybe you're right. It felt like all the time to me."

The waiter came back to take their dinner order. Euly ordered something light and Enaya, a steak with au gratin. She always had eaten what she wanted and it never seemed to show unlike Euly who was battling to keep her weight at bay through menopause.

"Where does it all go?"

"I work out."

After the day's travel, Euly felt a little tired plus the wine was making its way straight behind her eye sockets.

"Wine's good, isn't it?"

"They fought all the time."

"No they didn't."

"Yes."

"I don't remember it that way. I remember mother singing to me in the rocker and you playing with the neighbor boys. Remember that? Little Phil and Butchy? You guys always played Tarzan."

"Wow. I'd forgotten that and when you weren't sick, you were always Jane, remember?"

"Yeah." She laughed at the thought. They both did. "You changed."

"What do you mean?"

"You got all girly. Look at you. You're nothing like when we were kids."

"Neither are you."

"I don't know about that."

"You were always the little feminine princess, remember? Now, look at you. You look like a correspondent in Iraq with that vest and those readers on your head."

"Shut up!" Enaya had given her the verbal equivalent of a poke in the ribs.

"'Here, in Baghdad, the fighting heightens. The hovel behind me looks a lot like my office...'"

"Cut it out!"

"'And over here, in my kitchen, a car bomb has exploded, leaving a cabbage dead and hundreds of eggs injured.'"

"It's not like that anymore. I'm much neater."

"Right."

"Really."

"Uh huh. You've changed. You used to be this tidy, neat-as-a-pin person and now, you don't care about that."

"Not true. I do care. But, there's not much I can do about it. I'm super busy these days what with mother and everybody, it seems as though dying and obits are constant. Cleaning is about the last thing I can get to. That and dinners."

"Ohmygod. The gourmet chef cooks no longer?"

"Will you give it a rest."

"We all change, Eu. It's no big thing. I love everything just so. I used to be a slob. Big deal. There are many 'used to be's' in the world. What really matters is who we are today. Are we kind? Are we loving? That's all that really matters. Did we love?"

"I suppose." She used her standard answer when she didn't have a good comeback for her sister.

CHAPTER SEVENTEEN

After dinner, Euly waved her sister goodbye from inside the lobby entrance. She couldn't help but laugh when the valet brought around Enaya's Mercedes. She watched her tip the boy. Enaya stood like Vanna White, winked at her and with a flip of her head she got into her sleek car. Euly laughed and rolled her eyes and they both blew a kiss goodnight to each other, Euly through a glass door of a hotel and Enaya through her glass window.

A full day of traveling made her eyes heavy as she watched Enaya's car drive out of sight. She smiled and turned to go to her room.

Once there, she figured it was time she call her husband. After kicking off her shoes she sidled up onto the bed and leaned against her pillows. She dialed Geoff. After the third ring, she figured he would pick up. After the sixth, she hung up. She tried the number again thinking she dialed wrong and let the phone ring ten times before giving up.

Geoff hadn't mentioned he wouldn't be home, had he? She racked her brain trying to remember what he had said before she got onto the plane but couldn't remember him saying anything − not if he was going out, not anything. She only remembered their spat before leaving for Belle's, about the car door, and how anxious she'd felt. Geoff could've been the bellboy for all she remembered of that morning. She remembered her cell phone.

The display on her cell showed she had one message. Punching in the code she listened. Her face got hot in anger. From what he'd said, he had been trying her most of the day but she had forgotten to turn on the phone. Barely ever using it made it easy for her to forget about the thing. Their home sat in a crater of a dead zone and most often she used her land line. It was rare she bothered with the cell. It was meant for emergencies, really, and travel. It slipped her mind.

When he was finished firing angry remarks at her, he hung up. She saw the phone in the room was blinking. There was a message there too. It was a similar hateful tirade that she needed to call him fast.

"Okay. So, I'm calling you back. Where are you this time? And, why isn't the answering machine picking up?" The words bounced onto the empty walls of her room and fell onto the floor unanswered. It was close to eleven. She was exhausted and would deal with him in the morning.

CHAPTER EIGHTEEN

"I can't believe you forgot to turn your phone on again. How difficult is it, Euly." He covered the mouthpiece with his hand so he wouldn't say anything he regretted into his cell. He breathed out hard, "Call me when you get this message."

His feet pounded against the concrete walkway outside Belle's window. He paced in front and gazed in at her watching the doctors and nurses aspirate her lungs. This wasn't good. She was beginning to go through that suffering-stage the doctors had warned them about before. And, where was his wife? She should be here with her mother not somewhere off in Phoenix for God knows what.

He jammed the cell phone into his pocket and held it there in his left hand.

He bent forward to look through the window as his mother-in-law. Her convulsive cough seemed exaggerated to him as he witnessed the nurse insert a tube into her trachea and withdraw any excess fluids that were in her lungs. At one point, she looked as if she were going heave. He felt an automatic reaction to gag when he saw her choke and gasp. Geoff held his hand up to his mouth and looked away. He loved Belle. It wasn't easy to see her this way.

The smell of diesel floated in. It hung on the trail of a garbage truck that drove into the parking lot near the dumpster. It seemed late in the day to be picking up garbage. He looked down the walkway where an old man walked his wheelchair with his feet in front as he sat. He looked like a decrepit toddler in some oversized stroller. He smiled a toothless closed grin that sunk into his face. Geoff tipped his head up in recognition.

"Hello young fella."

"Good evening, sir."

"Cool tonight."

"Yep." He rubbed his arms across his body using both hands. "Better go in. Night."

"Night." The man rolled slowly off past Belle's window making his way on his usual route around the building and most likely back to his room.

Geoff rubbed his hands together. It was cold this afternoon. He headed back in and resolved to stay with Belle. She needed him tonight. It was too cold to be alone.

CHAPTER NINETEEN

"Mr. Jenkins isn't in at the moment. He said he had an appointment." The receptionist at Clive Jenkin's office looked at Euly with an unconcerned air about her. The busy tapping of typewriters behind her filtered through the room and gave a hurried pace to the small card company's office.

"Shoot. I'm in town for only a few days and I need to speak with him." She paused to see if the overly made-up buxom young red-head would respond. When she only looked with a blank stare back, Euly continued. "Do you know when he might be back?" Euly tried to smile but it felt forced.

"No. Maybe you can check back around two." She sat with slumped shoulders. Her low-cut tight jersey top revealed the girl's smashed cleavage.

They looked like oversized water balloons and were ready to pop. Euly wondered about her IQ.

"Okay, here." Fumbling in her purse she pulled out a card and handed to the receptionist. "Can you give this to Mr. Jenkins, Clive? It's my business card. It's rather important." She hoped the girl would see how much she needed to speak with Clive.

"You can call, you know."

The girl's comment stopped Euly in her tracks. She felt a surge of heat rise up and into her face but she caught herself when she sensed her body press forward. She wanted to reach out and grab the girl's blouse, twist it hard and get eye-to- eye with her but, instead, she said, "Okay. Thanks.

I'll check back later." When she turned to leave, Euly rolled her eyes and pushed out though the door.

"Yes. I came by earlier looking for Mr. Jenkins." Euly's voice trailed off into the phone and she paused expecting more disappointment but this time when she got legitimate helpful information she was happily caught off guard. "Oh! Oh, well, great. Where is that again?" Euly scratched the address onto a scrap of paper the hotel provided for its guests. "Great. Thank you." She looked at the address again and the name of the establishment where she could find Clive. It was Benny's.

She closed the door of the rented car. Euly could make out a faint trail of cigar smoke seeping out the seams of Benny's. Spotty gravel that covered the bar's parking lot crushed under Euly's boots. She walked forward on her toes to avoid abrading the leather heels. Between the concrete doorstep and the gravel weeds grew up in dry yellow clumps. There were cigarette butts and wrapping papers strewn about outside of the door. A concrete pad showed the shape of an etched-in fan on it from years of sustained use. The name of the bar was hand painted on its iodine metal door in black marker. Nothing looked different. Low on the heavy metal door was a dent. Directly next to the dent on the block outside were new bricks where old ones had been replaced. Two high windows in the front were painted out in light yellow which gave an eerie strobe-like effect on the inside. Euly yanked at the door and when it opened it scraped hard against the pad adding another moment in time to the fan in the concrete. Euly noticed the stench first − a farrago made up of urine and vomit, beer, whiskey and tobacco. As if protecting herself, she raised her hand to her mouth.

The dim insides made it feel like walking into a crypt. She realized she'd stopped breathing. The temperature was at least twenty degrees cooler than outside and she felt her nipples knot almost instantly. She pulled her purse strap over her shoulder in an attempt to hide her chest. She hadn't worn a sweater over her red-striped jersey shirt and she hoped the red striping concealed her tightening breasts. The days in Phoenix were still reaching close to the 90s and being from the northwest, she didn't expect to be cold there but she was never prepared for Benny's.

While her eyes adjusted, voices that had once been talking slowed and stopped as people inside the place took note of her. She made out the bar to the right and several grizzly men gathered at the far end, a couple sitting around Formica tables and a few more bodies standing near a solitary pool table.

"It's like seeing a ghost."

She barely remembered the smoky voice that spoke but looked in the direction it came from and asked, "Clive?"

"Who else, kid?"

"I can barely see you."

"We like it that way. Come on over to the bar and sit down."

She could still turn around and leave. No one in there but Clive knew her. She could still get away.

Clive was one of the group of men at the end of the bar.

She tugged at the hem of her blouse pausing for a mere second then stepped forward and walked over to him. His hair was still the curled mess she remembered but the gray had completely confiscated the black it used to be. He looked his age and Euly figured he must now be in his late sixties. Still he was the first to comment.

"You sure got old."

"Gee, Clive. You still look the same."

He chuckled at her apparent sarcasm. "Want a drink?" Euly nodded she did. "What'll it be?"

"Dalwhinny's." She needed to appear sure of herself and ordering the expensive scotch was the first thing that came to mind.

"Damn. Your father taught you right. One Dalwhinny's for the lady, and I'll have another." Euly wondered how many "another" was for Clive but he seemed to be holding his own. The man could drink she remembered that about him.

"Wow. How long has it been?"

"You want to play guessing games, Euly? Is that why you came to see me after all these years, for guessing games?" A couple of the men moved out of their stools away from the bar and took up seats farther away from them around an empty table. Euly followed their movement through the length of the mirror on the backsplash until they sat. She realized Clive was watching through the mirror also but he was watching Euly. Her eyes connected with his for a second and then darted off in a different direction. She noticed his body jerk as if he'd chuckled.

The bartender brought Euly's drink and she took a quick sip. The scotch acid burnt her throat as it traveled into her stomach. She took another sip and set the drink down.

"So, what do I owe the pleasure?" It seemed to Euly Clive had turned into a bundle of clichés. She reached into her bag to turn on the recorder. Her hand rummaged through her purse and she remembered taking it out and setting it on the desk in her hotel room. She'd left it there.

"I'm a writer, like you, Clive." Trying to cover any residual discomfort she felt, she stroked back her hair. "I'm writing a memoir. In fact, I brought a photo I thought you might help me with, to see if you remember anything from it." She pulled the photo out and handed it to Clive.

"Slow down, a minute. You're a writer?" He said it as if the possibility was out of grasp for him but examined the photograph. He set it down on the bar between them and turned to his cocktail. She picked it off the counter and slipped it back between some pages of her journal.

"Yes. Do you remember that party?" She tried to divert his attention back to the photo.

"*You*'re a writer." Clive seemed intrigued by her choice in careers.

"Is the idea so far-fetched?"

"It's not that, no honey. I just didn't expect it is all. Last I remember, you were riding a horse around all day long."

"Oh, my God. That's right when I was, what,

fifteen, sixteen? I had a horse back, well, you know."

"Yes you did. You were quite the little cowboy as I recall. Remember?"

Euly chuckled and they finally smiled at each other.

"Jeez. Clive, where have all the years gone? It seems like I could close my eyes and I'd be back."

"Hold on, Dorothy. Home isn't what you remember it to be. The hurricane done took the

house away." His reference to The Wizard of Oz made Euly wonder how bad it could've gotten for him.

"How so?"

"Things are shit now. That's how so."

"It's that bad?"

"It's worse." He polished off his cocktail and held up his glass for another.

Euly stared at him but only because she was lost in a memory trying to figure out where it must've gone bad for Clive. She assumed it was around the time Sandy died, her suicide attempts and then success.

"You miss her, Clive?" Euly asked in a low voice and as she asked she looked at her own drink to give him some room with the question.

"Oh, sure. Sure, I miss her. But, Euly, she left me long before she ever left this earth. She left me years before that." He took a mouthful of his cocktail.

"You mean because of dad and she?"

"What are you talking about, kid?"

"You know." She looked at Clive and raised her eyebrows in an effort to prompt him. He'd been drinking but he couldn't have possibly forgotten the thing that broke up Euly's parents. She didn't want to have to spell it out for him. She was embarrassed about all of it but he shook his head. "You know, the indiscretion?" She tried to egg him on with the word.

"Which one, kid?"

Euly stalled when he replied and then went on. "You know, Clive. The one between dad and Sandy." She couldn't believe she had to say.

He looked into his glass like he was trying to find something and jiggled the ice.

"Don't tell me you didn't know..."

"Know what? That Sandy and Ray had an affair?" His voice reared in a sort of contra- accusation.

"Well, yes. It broke up my family, for Christ's sake, Clive. It's exactly what I'm talking about."

He began shaking his head and grinning like Euly didn't know what the hell she was talking about. He took another gulp but continued to shake his head in disbelief. Then he turned back to her and went on.

"No, kid. That's not the way the story goes." He was refuting a well-known fact. "Man." He continued to shake his head and smirk.

"What?" Euly was losing her patience with his smug know-it-all-detective-façade. "What." The word came out more like a groan than a request. "No, kid." When he said it again, Euly's eyes rolled away from him and she breathed out. She was losing her patience with his morose drama.

"Your father was a saint, kid. He'd do nothing like that to your mother." The way Clive talked irked Euly and she couldn't help but feel she was having a conversation with Sam Spade. "Face it, kid, things were tough back then don't get me wrong. We all had troubles – double digit interest, soaring inflation, people out of work, desperation was thick in the air. But, it was nothing so bad your father would've done something like that to your mother." She didn't understand what Clive was telling her, all she could hear was the noise of his comic-book-delivery. Clive slammed back his whiskey and tapped the shot glass on the counter for the barkeep to bring him one more. Euly sipped at her drink and watched the bartender pour Clive's straight into his glass.

"Ice?" Clive shrugged him off so the guy left the bottle in front of him on the bar.

"She killed herself, Clive. It's not your fault.

She felt bad about what she did to you."

"It wasn't over me, kid, I can tell you that."

"Sandy loved you, Clive. You two were so

great together and she adored you. At least that's what I saw when you two came over. She'd come over and talk to mother too. I'd hear Sandy saying how much she loved you. Mother and Sandy were very close, Clive. I know she loved you plus I remember mother telling me that a couple doesn't have to be married to be in love."

"Look, I've said all I'm going to say about it. The past is the past. Who needs it anyway? The dead should stay six feet under where they belong. At your age you should be thinking about the present. Like now, the future comes way too fast." Clive turned to face her and then grabbed her arm. "Say, I have an idea. Why don't we blow this place and head on back to your hotel. We can order up some room service and tangle up the bed for a throw or two. What d'ya say, Euly. I'll tell you everything you want to know." It was obvious he hadn't forgotten anything between them like she'd hoped. She nearly got sick from his suggestion.

"That's not going to happen, Clive." Euly wrenched her arm but he wouldn't let go of his grip.

"Stop it, Clive. I'm married now."

"Right. Right." It was like he didn't believe it or that she cared.

"Happily!"

He blew out air from his nose and turned away. He released her arm and leaned against the bar. He swirled his drink in front of him, looking into it trying to find something else to say.

"Look, Clive. I'm doing some research about my past for my memoir. If you don't want to help, I'm not going to force you. Still, whether you or I like it or not, we're part of each other's past and I was hoping you might want to, help. That's all."

Clive's mood changed almost instantly and he lashed out at Euly.

"Why would I want to help you?" He bit out the question and returned his attention to his glass and got quiet. "Why don't you just go away and forget about it?" There was a sadness in his voice she couldn't miss. He picked up the bottle again and poured the drink that he needed to put him over the edge. Euly's body temperature kicked in and a wave of sudden heat covered her. She became physically agitated when she realized what her questions, moreover, what her presence had done to him. It seemed to kick him in the stomach. But, his mood flipped again. It was the liquor.

"Look, I don't want to go there with you, okay. It's over! Done with! Now, get out of here, kid. Go back home to your safe little life. I've got business to attend to."

He gestured to the room. "Go, get out of here!" He slammed the drink back and leaned against the bar as though he'd would fall down if the counter wasn't there.

Euly set her half-drunk whiskey onto the counter and stood up next to him. She patted Clive's back.

"Okay, Clive. Okay."

He was damaged goods. She almost laughed when she heard the term enter her head. Clive lived in a movie of his own making and she felt he might be rubbing off on her.

CHAPTER TWENTY

He watched the door scrape closed as she walked out of her life the way she did before. How'd she track him down, that's what he wanted to know. That big-mouthed stupid broad at the office, most likely gave her the name, place and times she could find him. He couldn't say anything to the slut because she was banging the boss. She'd take her complaints right to the old man and he'd be out of a job, again.

And, where had she found that photo? It was like seeing the whole day right there before him. Sandy looked so beautiful, so young. Belle looked mean as usual, pretty and mean, Moon and Teddy – happy as always and, clueless. Maybe not. Who knows. Who knows what happened that long ago, who knew what, why or what really happened. Euly was kicking up old dry dirt, kicking it into his face and he was getting pissed sitting there at the bar.

He knew he loved Sandy back then, more than anything in the world. Euly was a distraction afterward. But, Sandy was the love of his life and it all fell apart.

He sat shaking his head and mumbling until the bartender came up and jostled him. He didn't realize he was saying anything, doing anything.

"Oh lord." He said it loud enough for people to turn in their chairs. "Oh, lord. Get me another one, quick." The thoughts flooded back over him. "I think you've had enough Clive."

"Give me one more drink, Benny. Dammit. Now!"

Benny poured the drink light and set it down in front of him. "You need to leave after this one, Clive. Drink it and go."

He pulled out his money and threw it at him. Clive grabbed the shot and pounded it back. He smacked his lips. "Ahh. That should do 'er." He stood up and stumbled hard, knocking over the

stool and almost falling. He wavered but picked up the stool and righted it and put a finger to his lips. "Shh. Noisy, noisy." He whispered.

Benny shook his head and pointed for him to leave. "You get busted driving and it's my ass, Clive."

"I won't get busted. Hell, I'm gonna drive home as fast as I can just to avoid the police." He clicked his teeth and winked at Benny. He gunned a slow-motion John Wayne finger at him. Clive knew he could smooth talk anyone.

"Just go, Clive."

"I looked at the moon and then I looked at June and, alas, the moon was prettier than June." – Jay Adams, radio personality (1927 to 1996)

CHAPTER TWENTY ONE

She could hear the locks being unlatched from inside the house and after much jarring the door finally opened. A slim elderly woman stood before her. Aunt Moon had aged but Euly would've been able to recognize her across a football stadium.

She'd remember anywhere that perfect thin long nose and her high cheek bones that flared out like a tulip to frame her big dark eyes. Her hair had gone all but white and still in a stylish coif that spoke of cash, cash on hand. She remembered the money many Lebanese families brought back from the old country.

Euly was amazed at her aunt's self-sufficiency, her independence, from the time she was only a young woman and at a time when the same expectations were more inclined to the opposite sex. She and Uncle Teddy divorced around the same time her parent's had.

It made sense now knowing what she knew about Micaiah.

She couldn't broach the subject immediately.

Euly had to ease into it smoothly.

"I made some baba especially for your visit." Her aunt wrapped her arms around her neck and hugged her out on the porch.

"No way! I love your baba, auntie. It's the best."

"You always did love my cooking. You were such a good girl. It looks like some things never change."

And, charming. She was the same charming woman she'd grown up around. Euly felt a pang rush through her. It was the first time she'd ever felt a longing to be back in Phoenix.

"Well, you haven't seen me in ten years, auntie, maybe I've become a horrible, bitter woman." She waved a dismissive hand at her and smiled.

"Life is hard. It wouldn't surprise me if you've changed a little."

Euly couldn't gauge from her facial expression but she felt invisible. She felt as though Aunt Moon knew exactly why she'd come back to visit her. Euly lowered her eyes when her aunt looked at her.

"Would you like some Arak? I still have some." Euly looked up fast and smiled. There was a glint in her eye and a curl at the side of her mouth.

"Good lord, you don't."

Her aunt beamed and shook her head furiously. She was giddy about the suggestion and got two cordials out before Euly could even respond.

"Well, if you insist." Euly grinned a wide sweeping grin when she could see her aunt was acting like a kid. "Do you know how long it's been since I've had Arak?"

"I'm guessing it's been a while. Probably not since your dad." She turned and tipped her head in an apology. Her aunt's mention of him flipped Euly head-over-heels to somewhere other than where she was right then and there. It was a time-warp.

CHAPTER TWENTY TWO

She remembered her dad with a cigarette hanging out of his mouth. It was cool to smoke back when cigarettes weren't killers, when they were filter-less and advertised on TV — Lucky Strikes,

Camels and Marlboros. Throughout her mother's albums, Euly found photo after photo of him in his Army uniform with a cig dangling sloppily from his bottom lip and her dad saying something funny to the camera man. Another one: the cigarette, her sister still in diapers, and Ray holding Enaya up proudly with a smoke sandwiched in a tight wide grin looking like a small erection. That was her dad, Ray — available for any photo op, quick-witted, dashing in his youth — the smoker.

Belle drew him once, his face. Euly adored that portrait and confiscated it after her father's death. People always commented to Euly about that drawing. They said how much her dad reminded them of Paul Newman when Newman was a young man but dad was darker, much darker, and Euly was sure Mr. Newman didn't understand the word hummus the way her dad understood it, as a staple in his diet, a part of every meal from infant to adult.

He grew up in the Depression Years and fought in World War II and the Korean War, consecutively. He loved the Army and talked about it all the time. He carried the Army's teachings into his civilian life by shining his shoes daily. And, she knew when was shining his shoes. The potent polish permeated the house and wafted into her bedroom.

The soft swishing as he buffed resonated through her door like a whisper or a glass against the wall.

He made a bed you could bounce a quarter off of, and kept his toiletries in a small satchel, just in case he had to leave quickly. He had his satchel stocked and ready the day he died. That day she opened a can of Ray's shoe polish and let its leathery fragrance saturate her senses. And, Old Spice cologne – Old Spice and Ray went hand in hand. One was nothing without the other.

Ray told Enaya and Euly stories about the guys he spent time with during his service. Pride beamed from him when he spoke about his barrack- mates in Washington at Fort Lewis. He told the girls tales of camping in the woods and sleeping in his "fart sack" on Mount Rainier during weekend trainings. Many years after, when Euly was seventeen, he wrote and told her once about the experience. It was the first time she recalled ever hearing the story. He'd sent the letter when she and her sister were traveling the Pacific Northwest one summer. Enaya was twenty. And it was funny they were in the same stomping grounds their father had beat during boot camp and when he was around their same age.

Ray made his money when he opened Romano's, an Italian restaurant. A few years afterward, he opened another one across town. Until, he had a chain of Romano's around the

valley. And, although the restaurants were extremely successful, Ray retained an unpretentious style and was a comedian at heart.

Ray was born in 1927 to Euly's grandfather who left Lebanon and all his cash in a dash — at least that's the way the story went. Even though Euly had not one photo of the man, she remembered her grandfather to be grim and reclusive.

Ray was the middle son and seemed to have an insatiable need to be in the spotlight. He made silly faces, cracked jokes, pushed cigarettes into one side of his nose like a magic trick and dragged them out the other, or stuck burned-out flashbulbs into one or both of his nostrils to make it look like he had bubbles of snot hanging out. The girls found his capers uproariously funny because he wanted to make people laugh. But, Ray's father found little humor in his antics.

Ray grew up to be sweet and gentle. It was odd due to his upbringing by a hardened man with a mysterious past. When he died, Ray was crushed. He died before giving Ray the approval he so desperately hungered for, a hunger only his father could sate. And, to this day, Euly wondered if her grandfather was proud of Ray for serving in the Army. Ray died of congestive heart failure. The doctors attributed it to his smoking. The recollection of her family felt hard like sharp pebbles under bare feet.

Their family did normal middle-class family things together — went to Disneyland, Carlsbad Caverns, took road trips, sang in the car, fixed BBQs in the backyard, swam in a manufactured metal swimming pool, owned a dog and a cat, had training wheels on their bikes with flags of pink and yellow ribbon streamers from the handle bars. They grew up like Joe America. She had nothing to complain about and yet.

For her, it seemed the world was racing by and her legs were feeling leaden. Up to now she'd had nominal successes in life — was one of the lucky ones.

He left them once just before her eighteenth birthday. It was 1975. Belle forced him out. He'd let the family down with his "indiscretion." When it happened, she lashed out, rebelled, cut off her jeans like a leftover hippy, smoked pot, and messed around with a boy in the costume room behind the school's theatre all before her parent's divorce settlement.

Back further, to the early 60's, dust storms rolled into the desert basin like a tsunami over innocent beaches raping the land. The storms were some of her earliest childhood memories. She remembered lying on her back, her mother pumping the rocking chair under them and watching through a screen-door a brewing storm rage out past the tops of neighborhood houses, out past a low line bowl of sage scented mountains, out past the ends of earth for all she could see through the door, there on her mother's lap. The vision crystallized in her mind.

Euly would lie on her back when afternoons dipped into evening, after dinner time when no one else was home – not dad, not Enaya. She drank chocolate milk out of a coke bottle made with Nestlé's powdered chocolate and ice cold whole milk. Belle mixed it in green Coke bottles. She remembered her mother holding the bottle with one thumb pressed over the opening and shaking it to mix the ingredients. Belle would lick her thumb and hand the bottle over to Euly. It was their ritual. The earlier Euly could remember, the more pleasant the visions became however finite.

And, Belle, tortured with a fear of thunder storms, let her fear bleed out onto her girls. She was born at a time when the heat played tricks on people's eyes — when mirages slid across the earth like ghosts, when stargazers could watch Leo prowl the evening sky. Her mother, sick and tired of the pregnancy, released Euly late one day in the middle of August.

That day, a coming storm played havoc on Belle's nerves. That's what she told her girls — Euly was born in the middle of a storm.

CHAPTER TWENTY THREE

Euly's mind snapped back to Moon's words. "Oh, my God. Of course, I remember." Aunt

Moon's comment shook Euly out of her trance. She spoke in a quieter voice. "I remember those parties, Eu." She seemed to detect Euly's mood and nearly whispered after her first sip of Arak.

"Not those parties, auntie, that party, the last one. Don't you remember?"

"Oh my, yes. It was horrible. That poor little girl."

"Well, auntie, I'm trying to find out as much information about her as possible. I'm writing my memoir and wanted to start the story there, at that time in my life."

"A memoir? Isn't that fascinating."

"Well, I hope so." She looked hard at her aunt. "Mother told me some things about that party, other things, that I wanted to verify with you."

"Well, I'm sure she remembers it well. It was a very sad day." She shook her head as she remembered. "You know her brother died just before they moved out here."

"That's what you told me when I called. It's awful."

Aunt Moon shook her head as she suckled her drink.

"Have some baba." She spooned the dip out onto a plate and loaded Euly up with pita bread. She slathered dip onto one of the pieces of bread and shoved half of it into her mouth. The lemon was first to hit her then the garlic. The salty flesh of the eggplant melted over her tongue and she rolled her eyes.

"Oh, auntie, it's just like I remember.

Wonderful."

"Well, we have lots. Eat. You need to eat." She now understood how her body had gotten the curves it had today.

"What happened to them – the girl's family?"

"Well, the father died of heart failure not long after, maybe a year, no, it was more like two or three years after the little girl drowned. And, the oldest brother fell to pieces. He became a drunk and I think he even did marijuana. So sad."

"Is the mother still alive?"

"Oh, yes. I see her occasionally still at the Cedar Club. She is a strong woman. Had to be, I suppose. What else can you do? She only had one child left but you stay alive for that one, you know? Can't take your own life. God doesn't look happily on that." She picked up a piece of bread and scooped up a dollop of baba, folded it into her pita and ate the whole thing in one bite.

"I can't imagine. I know I haven't had any children of my own but, still, I just can't see how someone can live through that." As she spoke it, she realized how her aunt must feel about the subject. "Oh, auntie. I'm sorry. I'm being so careless about your feelings."

"No dear. No need to apologize. I love thinking about my darling Micaiah. He was a gentle boy."

"It must be so painful."

"It is. Even after this long. I cry every single day." Her eyes began to well up and she stared straight at Euly, almost freezing in place.

"Mother told me some things, you know."

She charged forward hoping to distract her aunt from crying.

"About what, dear." She dabbed her nose with her napkin.

"About when you all were younger. Silly things. Irresponsible things."

"Well, we were kids too, you know. We made mistakes."

Euly stopped talking and ate a couple more bites before getting her nerve. "You and dad were close."

"He was an angel. We were best friends, Eu."

"You dated before mother and he were married, isn't that right?"

"Ancient history. It was only for about a year.

Then he met your mother and that was that."

"I thought you broke it off after you met Uncle Teddy."

"It all happened around the same time, honey. One left, the next showed up. It was a long time ago."

"Mother mentioned there might've been a little, oh god, how do I say this. Lag time between you and dad."

"Lag time? What do you mean?"

"You know, that it wasn't all the way over when mother came into the picture."

"That's not how I remember it. But, we were always close. We knew each other when we were kids grew up together. We moved down the block from your grandparent's house and Ray and his brothers were always around. You know, just kid stuff, until we got older, that is."

"Why would mother think there was something else?"

"Honey, how should I know? But, I don't remember anything else. I don't think I do. It all happened within a matter of months, as I recall. Belle showed up. Teddy showed up. I'm not sure who came first now that you mention it."

"It's kind of important to me, auntie."

"For your memoir, you mean?"

"No, well, yes that but also it's important to our family." Euly was fighting the urge to blurt out the question but was losing the battle.

"It's important to our family who came first – your mother or Uncle Teddy?"

"Well, no, not when you put it like that."

"Honey, what's troubling you?" Her aunt saw her frustration and Euly wondered if she were frowning. "Just ask me."

"Just ask you, huh?"

"Yes. What's so hard about that?" She set down her baba and leaned in.

"It's not like we were ever related, right? Not biologically, right?"

"No but we were as good as."

Euly leaned back in her chair and put her fork down. She grabbed her Arak and slugged it back.

"Euly. What is it?" Aunt Moon forced.

"Mother said that you and dad were not quite over with when you and Uncle Teddy got together and Uncle

Teddy married you because you were pregnant. There." She breathed out relief.

"What! Why would your mother say something like that!

"She said that Micaiah was my biological brother, my half-brother and that she wanted me to know that I had a brother before she died."

"Good God."

"So, what does that mean? Is it true or not?"

"It's most certainly not true."

"She said you would say that too."

"Oh, my God. Do you believe her?"

"She is my mother, auntie."

"She's lying."

"She said you might say that too, auntie and that you had the birth records to prove it."

Aunt Moon sat unmoving and stunned. Euly went on.

"She said that I should ask you to see Micaiah's birth record."

"There's nothing on his record that proves your father is Micaiah's father."

"So it's your word against my mother's."

"I suppose it is."

"Can I at least see the birth record?"

"If I can't prove the matter one way or the other then what's the point?"

"I just thought it would help me somehow."

"Help you how?"

"I don't know maybe I could be able to tell one way or the other."

"How about this, my dear, how about you request an exhuming, dig up my poor dead son's body, do one of those, uh, uh, DNA tests and find the truth out that way!" She stood. "You've more than worn out your welcome, young lady. You'd better go."

"Auntie. I'm sorry but if I could just see his birth certificate, I know I could tell."

"Now!" She lifted her arm and pointed to the door. "You have to leave. You come here and insult me like this after everything. I won't have it. Now, leave. This instant."

CHAPTER TWENTY FOUR

"She made me leave."

"It couldn't be your winning personality, could it?"

"What does that mean." It wasn't a question but a demand.

They were in the arms of an argument and she wasn't about to back down.

"Look, Euly. All I know is you have a way about you. That's all I'm going to say."

"A way."

"Yes. A way. And you never let up."

"You have no idea what even happened and you're telling me it's my fault."

"I can only imagine."

"You know, Geoff, if you could imagine you'd understand why I'm here and you're there. Goodbye." Officially, saying 'goodbye' meant she hadn't hung up on him. Geoff hated people hanging up on him, especially Euly. She remembered once when she had. He called back immediately and told her never to do it again. He added emphasis by telling her to pull her head out of her ass. At the time, it was funny. Now, however, it felt sickening. At dark crevice in the back of her mind, she couldn't believe she was married.

She felt as though they couldn't talk to each other anymore. Their conversation got off to a rough start and tumbled into a battle. She'd only intended to ask why he hadn't answered the phone but her question sounded contrived. His retort felt like an accusation. She ended the conversation wondering why she called at all. What she really wanted was to tell him she missed him, tell him about what happened with her aunt. She tried but he baited her.

CHAPTER TWENTY FIVE

The sun was warm through the hotel window where she dunked her tea bag into the steeping water. She was lounging and felt ill-prepared to start another day. She awoke with a sense of being unconnected. Her dreams were so out of line with her life. In this one, she was getting married to a younger man and had to break it off with her previous husband. These two people painted their walls creating a new environment meant to be creative and all about art. Janie, Euly's hairstylist, sat her in the chair, tipped her back in a freakish massage position meant to relax her before the cut. She sputtered whispers into Euly's ear as she leaned her backwards almost into a lying position. That's when Euly awoke feeling disoriented and in a bad mood.

It felt wrong. Meeting Clive had felt wrong.

Not because he'd made a pass at her although that was enough to make Euly not want to return but, something else. She couldn't put it together. She'd been preoccupied by his style and didn't always hear what he was saying, only how he was saying it. Damn. She was trying to remember his words. She cursed herself for having forgotten the recorder.

She knew she needed to talk to him once more and she dreaded it. He would take it as a come-on to his advances. They had history. Nothing serious but their history was enough to make him think her visit might be something more.

It was in college. He wanted to meet for cocktails.

"Just to talk." He laughed at the suggestion. To Euly, it meant more. He wanted to sleep with her. It was a time when sex was what you did on a date there was no feeling around under a blouse in fumbling for the clasp of a bra, bras were optional. By then, she had a place of her own. His place was with Sandy but only months before they divorced and a year before she killed herself.

"We can meet at Houston's and after that, I don't know. We could go to your place." After say 'yes,' Euly stood him up.

It was too weird even for her, even at that time in her life when she was a wild one. The late

70s were making a turn into the 80s. By then, she'd found herself fully imbued in the culture- free love and drugs.

CHAPTER TWENTY SIX

An absent moon made the night even darker. *Wild Thing* played on the radio. It was long ago, around the age of seventeen.

Euly put a hand over her eyes just thinking about it. She'd had sex with two boys at once. They tangled together, one boy below her hips and she at the other boy's groin. Every point of the business muddled into a mix of arms and legs, breasts and genitalia. No one spoke. They simply continued the process to its natural end.

It was during this interlude a thought struck her: life might not continue simply as it once had.

Her mind wandered. What made her do it — the act itself?

At this stage of her life, she couldn't remember the events leading up to it. It was so long ago. Still, through it all many things came to mind.

One foremost thought, was of the complicated human-animal urge.

That urge we succumb to in the latest hour, the darkest of places, through exhaustion or illumination — that urge.

The urge when you ask yourself, "why not?"

The urge that makes men leave their families for a sampling of something new. The visceral pang we cannot control, don't want to control.

That urge.

Another thing crossed Euly's mind, the notion of polygamy and how readily Christians reject the precept and remembering a Mormon girlfriend back then. She wondered, as the three fluxed in constant motion, in the throes of passion, if polygamy mightn't be a better choice.

However, after bodily fluids dried up and the glow had died away, Euly's feelings changed in distinct steps — feelings from the act itself, that glorious interlude to an eventual thank you and two goodbye kisses, to embarrassment and, then, to downright shame.

It made her think of a joke. The one about a doe that bounds out of the woods and breathlessly vows, "I'll never do that for two bucks again!"

She began to ponder the bible and Adam and Eve. The writings say that in the Garden of Eden after the consumption of the apple from the tree of knowledge of good and evil, Adam tells God, "I heard thy voice in the garden, and I was afraid, because I was naked, and I hid myself".

Yet, before eating the forbidden fruit, Eve and Adam bounded happily about stark raving naked, unaware of their form. Only did they, upon the advent of sin, when Adam ate the apple. At which point, they sew fig leaves into clothing and cover their parts. Anyway, in terms of the Bible, after the three-way she guessed she covered her parts.

Because of her upbringing — mass every Sunday and catechism every Saturday — she felt her innocence could dissipate overnight. The snake hangs in the tree.

Yet, over thirty years later, when she pondered that night and remembered the boys, she remembered it now with warmth and asked herself, "How can that be?" She wondered how such a seemingly disdainful act could lend itself to a feeling of tenderness? Can time feign penance? Today, the act seemed outside her as if it happened to someone else and she was merely the conduit for the story of that girl so long ago. Did she tell anyone? Hell no, she never uttered a word.

Could Clive have found out? Euly doubted it. But, even if Phoenix was a large city, it still had a small town feel. People were connected. People knew people. People had found out too much about her. She'd gotten away once and wondered if she could do it again this time.

What was the old adage? You can run but you cannot hide.

Their conversation jingled like pennies in a pocket, like someone walked by you while your head was down, like being unmissed. Had Clive alluded to something she didn't hear? She was usually quick to the draw on innuendo but felt like she'd missed important parts of their talk. Or, was she simply fabricating a way to add apprehension to another meeting with him.

It was years ago. They were younger. It didn't matter. He didn't care anymore. She couldn't get out from under the shadow of the bible when she played the era out in her mind. A trickle of sweat leaked from under her left breast, the larger one, and she wiped it off by stuffing her cotton pajama top into the fold of her skin. She hated this town.

CHAPTER TWENTY SEVEN

When no one answered, Euly went around to the side to check in the window of Aunt Moon's garage and found her car gone. She dropped her arms and looked one way then the other. She sighed. After speaking with Geoff about the visit, she wanted to apologize to her aunt for her behavior. She wanted to make amends and explain the loss she felt. She needed her aunt's forgiveness. She wanted to say it didn't matter anymore and she was sorry.

Her time in Phoenix so far was fraught with bad memories and bad habits. She opened her bag and grabbed a pen and paper. She would leave her message on her door by slipping it into the crack of the screen door. After writing it, she folded it one, twice, three times. If Aunt Moon wanted to, she could call Euly on her cell and they might be able to meet up again and, hopefully, make up. She hoped they would. Her aunt was a gentle elderly woman. She didn't want her aunt's last memories of her to be about their last visit together. Euly had no doubt she would forgive her for the way she acted yesterday and forgive the things she said.

Euly tried to force the note into the door's seam but it was too tight. She unfolded the note once and tried again but it didn't work. She unfolded the note to its single thickness but, still, she found the seam too tight. She grabbed the door handle and gave it a tug. It budged but not enough to loosen. She walked back around to the side of the house, toward the side again, and in back where she knew there was a door leading into the garage. Aunt Moon's yard was manicured even there on the side where she walked. A medley of mosaic stepping stones had been inset in the cool round leaves of Dichondra ground cover. There, on the shady side of the garage, her aunt hung baskets of geraniums and petunias that spilled over their cedar containers. Euly had to go through the redwood gate to get to the garage door where she'd have a better chance of slipping the note into one of its cracks.

The handle turned fully. It surprised her to find the door unlocked especially in Phoenix. She stepped inside. The emptiness of the room echoed when she shut the door. It felt like a museum. Inside the room held captive a confusion of car oil and gasoline mixed with detergent and softener. Euly stood silently next to the washer and dryer, the same ones she remembered when she romped

through the house as a girl. She looked at the brand, a heavy-duty old set from the 1960's and she smiled to think how they don't make things the way they used to. Next to those were three wicker laundry baskets stacked within each other. The top one still had a few crumpled and dingy rags and towels, kitchen towels, looking ready for a wash. The door to the house was just next to the laundry area. She felt awkward on the inside of her aunt's garage like an intruder. If that door was unlocked, she'd just place the note on the kitchen counter, just two steps inside, and leave. If it wasn't, she'd slip the note in the crack of the kitchen door. Euly prayed Aunt Moon didn't have an alarm.

The same familiar scent she'd noticed the day before hit Euly when the door swung open. It was a fragrance only Aunt Moon could produce, one of fennel and *Evening in Paris*, her favorite cologne. She stood inside thinking how comfortable she felt, how unusually comfortable like it was her home too. This was the house she, Enaya and Micaiah had played countless times. This was the home where they ran Tonka toy trucks over dirt mounds in the backyard and played hopscotch on the driveway with yellow pink and blue chalk smeared on their small hands and clothing. It was the same home where their two families spent eating breakfast, lunch and dinner together, opening presents at Christmas together right over there by the picture window the very one shaded the ponderosa pine outside. The pine the kids climbed. This was the same home where, just a day before, she'd questioned her aunt about Micaiah —

asking her to prove his birthright. She couldn't believe how badly it had gone. Still, Moon could've just as easily put her questions to rest by showing her. Was that so much to ask? A chill covered her when a blast from the air conditioner kicked on and blew on her neck. It reminded her of someone breathing down her neck. It startled her. She couldn't believe she had been so bold to come into her house.

The wooden slats of the old tambour desk slid easily into itself as she opened the lid. Each drawer contained orderly stacks of antique and yellowed papers kept within sepia-colored manila folders — each tabbed marking its contents — closer to the front of the drawer was one marked home remodel, another marked last will & testament, and so on until she came upon one marked vital records. Euly paused. Her heart quickened and she held her breath. She pulled out the manila folder and sat on the floor. She put one hand over it holding it down waiting to open it and keeping her hand ready to lift it out but stalling until she worked up the nerve.

The first bunch of papers was a stapled set containing Aunt Moon and Uncle Teddy's marriage certificate, next was of her aunt's and one of her uncles birth certificates. Directly behind those was Micaiah's birth information. She stopped and stared at the death certificate that had been the last thing stapled to his set. Her hand slid across the top of it almost caressing the cool sheet as she read the information her hand was passing over. He died so young. Her pulse quicken when she remembered what she was looking for. She lifted the death certificate.

CHAPTER TWENTY EIGHT

It was dreamlike, reading about him her brother, her cousin, whatever he was to her. It was a feeling like dog-paddling, everything muscle working at once yet suspended, unmoving. Or the reeling sensation, that impression of freedom as someone pushes you on a swing away clinging going forward and up, clinging as it returns. A familiar voice felt distant from where she sat on her spot of the floor but ringing true in her ears. The sharp shrill sound of a clarion seemed to ring in her ears, how many times? Once, twice, the third shattering into someone speaking, then words and became crystal clear when the woman called out to her the third time.

"Euly? What are you doing?"

It still didn't seem real. Her movement seemed out-of-body. She felt her head lifting and looking up and over her shoulder toward the sound but she was voiceless as she turned.

"What in God's name are you doing?" She repeated to her niece. "I, uh, I..."

"How did you get in here?" Aunt Moon's face crushed into a question and her eyes flared open.

"Oh my God. Aunt Moon."

"How did you get in?"

"Through the garage. The back door was open and the kitchen door..."

"What have you got?"

She didn't answer but lifted the folder up so she could see.

"Micaiah?" Her voice arced and sounded as though he'd just walked into the room after not seeing him in many years.

"Oh my God, auntie, I'm sorry."

She snatched the folder from her hands and flipped through to make sure nothing had been stolen.

"Leave."

"Auntie, I can explain."

"You can? You can explain how you broke into my home and went rummaging through my personal things? You can explain how you've violated my trust in you, violated the memory of my precious Micaiah? Leave."

"Auntie. I'm..."

"Leave!"

The rental car tires skidded when she put it into gear and drove off. Her hands shook violently. She fought a sudden urge to cry. Her head pounded. Her eyes ached from the pressure building behind them. How could she explain what she had done? What was she thinking?

She fumbled for the cell phone in her purse but whom would she call? Whom would she tell what had happened? Her mother would understand. It was her fault anyway. She'd try her mother.

CHAPTER TWENTY NINE

She understood the pull toward another person — the constant harping of fantasies rolling around in your head of another someone. It wasn't you wanted to be untrue, no, it was more a Pac- Man of thoughts — you wanted to consume someone else if only a little and for a short time until the desire cooled.

She'd heard men call it the conquest. For women, it was more of a collection. A little untidy something they could store high on a shelf and out of sight. She hadn't felt the urge in a long while and blamed menopause for the dullness in her body that had replaced more torrid sensations of youth.

She wore the vest she called her 'writer's vest', the one she'd intended to wear on her trip back to Seattle. It had lots of pockets for pads of paper and pens, her recorder. It was normal for the bar. The cool room was in stark contrast to the warm November day she walked out of when she entered Benny's again. A fading spotlight shone behind her and faded as the closing door sliced the light away. The cigar smoke was thick, thicker than before, and she felt saliva building in the back of her throat.

How could people do this to themselves? She removed her sunglasses and spotted Clive sitting in the same spot at the bar humped over his glass. He didn't look up, he didn't speak this time because he wasn't expecting her. He was leaning on both elbows with a cigarette in his left hand. He held the thing like a woman, deep in the crotch sandwiched between two fingers.

Only when she set her bag on the bar next to him did he look at her, over his right arm.

"You're back." He didn't act surprised. He didn't act angry. He acted as if he quite expected it but could have gone his entire life without seeing her again.

"I'm back." She slid up onto a stool. "There are some things you said and I need to understand what you meant." She reached into a pocket and without pulling it out, played with each angle of the recorder until she found the on button.

"Yeah, like what?" He took a drag off his cigarette and blew it out up over his head.

"Well, first off, why exactly did you and Sandy split?"

"And, that would be your business, how?"

"Come on, Clive, it's, as you said yourself, ancient history. How can it hurt you now?"

Clive was on his third or fourth drink and beginning to eye the bartender for another. Euly couldn't help to think how the past must have contributed to his current demise, his daily alcoholic lunch. She felt sorry for him and disgusted all at the same time.

"Euly. You have no idea what you're asking."

"All I'm asking is for you to come clean. Tell me what split you guys up. It's been, what, nearly forty years and you can't talk about it, still?" She couldn't understand. "Look, Clive, Bill and I were unfaithful to the point of being ridiculous but it's over. That was only ten years ago and even I can talk about that. He screwed around on me and it hurt so I hurt him back. How can your story be any different? What could possibly be so bad?"

Clive rubbed a hand over his entire face.

"Lord, you're just not going to give up on this one, are you?"

Euly shook her head and stared hard into his eyes and held his gaze. She wasn't about to lose their connection.

"Another, Clive?" The bartender wasn't helping his condition any and poured him another drink. He asked, "More ice?"

"No, I'm good."

He almost seemed to forget she was there. When she adjusted her position, he tipped his head in her direction.

"So." Her question swung high in the air.

"So, so." He frowned. "I can see why you got a divorce. You say you got married again, did you?"

"Look Clive, you can insinuate all you want but it's not going to change the reason why I'm here. Just tell me. I'll leave right after that. You won't have to deal with me ever again."

"Didn't you say you were writing a memoir?"

"I'm changing the names to protect."

"It wouldn't be me you'd need to protect."

"Now, see, that's what I'm talking about.

What does that mean?"

"Just what I said." He knew he had baited

her and took a long slow drag from his cigarette. He blew a gray stream just as long in front of him. It traveled until it hit the back wall of the bar and tumbled within itself.

"You love this toying with people don't you? You know, screw you, Clive. I don't need your stinking side of things. There are others who remember you and Sandy. They'll tell me what they think happened and I'll use their information, whether it's true or not. It's my flippin' story. I'll tell it the way I want."

"You sure are sparky, Euly. Why didn't I ever get any of that?" He patted her thigh.

"Quit, Clive." She swiveled her legs away from him. "Cut it out."

"Why'd you stand me up back then?" And that was it, the whole reason he wasn't giving her what she wanted now.

"Well, for one, you were more like my uncle than a guy I would date."

"No, that's not it. You were always a flirty little thing with me. I wasn't too old for you. So, what was it?"

"I don't know, Clive." Air fluttered from her lips. "I just couldn't bring myself to. It seemed taboo or something. I don't know."

"Taboo, huh?"

"I guess." Euly lowered her eyes and unraveled the memory – the phone call, her acceptance and then not showing up. But, she had accepted and felt guilty for it.

"You were next on my list, kid. I wanted you so bad."

"Clive, please."

"Let's go to the hotel. Who would know but us?"

"Answer my questions, Clive." Euly's lips curved up.

She could've added, *That's why I'm here. No other reason than that!* But she didn't. She let his question lay open. She allowed him a shred of hope. Enough of a shred for him to bite.

"The game's afoot, then?"

"Something like that." She couldn't believe she was letting him believe she'd have sex him for the information but there she was doing just that. He smiled at her.

"Okay. Cool. Let me buy you a drink first."

CHAPTER THIRTY

Euly wiped her nose and sniffed. The phone rang and startled her and although she was worried it might be Clive, she picked up the phone anyway.

"Hello."

It was Geoff. He was telling her she sounded like she was getting a cold. He was telling her they needed to talk about the separation — how they needed not to do anything rash, to think about everything that was happening in their lives, maybe even go get counseling. He seemed worried but the knock on the door startled her.

"Crap." She whispered it, forgetting Geoff was listening. He asked her what was wrong. When she said it was nothing he didn't believe her and kept pressing her to tell him.

"It's nothing. I just wasn't expecting it. That's all." She didn't realize she was still whispering and when he broached that point, she lashed out at him but still held her whisper. "Look, is this an interrogation or something? I don't need this, Geoff."

Whoever was on the other side of the door knocked again.

"I've got to go. I'll call you..." Before she could finish, Geoff's end of the line went dead. "Dammit."

She looked through the peephole but saw no one. With her back against the door she could feel her body shaking. Her left hand involuntarily made its way up to her mouth but rather than chew at a nail she rocked her thumbnail hard in-between a bicuspid and an incisor to the point of making a dent in it.

Her head thronged in pain--the crying, the worry and, now, this thing with Geoff. She fumbled into her luggage. An old thin tube of Anacin peeked through the mesh compartment. Geoff had left it there from a weekend trip to Seattle they'd taken, right after his knee surgery a couple years back.

She quickly unzipped the compartment and pulled out the tube. The cap was difficult to turn but she managed, even with shaking hands. For some reason, the pills didn't look right. They looked like the old style of aspirin, without a coating for easy swallowing.

Still, Euly popped two into her mouth. They tasted tart and bitter. She filled a glass with water and shook her head once to help guide the pills down her throat. The headache felt like it might accelerate into a full-blown migraine so she emptied out one more pill into her palm and took that one too.

She made her way back to the door and looked again through the peephole. Whoever had knocked, had left.

Balancing her rump on the edge of the bathtub she watched the water filling the tub. A soak would help her relax. While she waited, the small room filled with mist.

Not waiting for the tub to fill, she dipped one toe in and laid back. The warm water rushed over her stomach and breasts, finally pouring up and over her shoulders, reclining fully and placing her feet onto the faucet wall, raised, straight-legged at an angle.

But, then, a moment of dizziness enveloped her. It was a singular whoosh. Her head began to feel thick and uncomfortable. The sound of water filling ricocheted within the room, almost too loudly.

She sat up but crumbled back to a recline when she found it difficult to breath.

The dizziness remained but now a buzzing began deep inside her ears.

She began to breathe heavily. Her breathing quickened and her chest felt tense. She tried to sit up again lifting her arms above her head, trying to stretch out her ribcage but instead felt the dizziness overtake her, crumbling yet again, lying in the tub. Her legs weak and useless, flopped openly held up only by the sides of the bathtub.

Trying to normalize her rugged breathing, Euly sucked back deep pockets of air, holding them but nausea set in.

Feeling as if she was being held down, she struggled to get up. But, the water splashing against the walls of the tub echoed in her head like a bongo throughout the tiny room. She flopped her arms over the sides but then only hung there.

The nausea gripped her again and she fell back into the tub lying back.

Her eyes wanted to close. A helpless feeling to sleep wrapper around her as she lay there, the water running, but an irresistible urge to close her eyes took over, like a gripping around the neck, and as she sank lower, Euly fell unconscious.

CHAPTER THIRTY ONE

Enaya closed her car door and looked up just as a man pushed his way, hard, out from the lobby doors.

He stomped across the parking lot and got into his car. He started the car but didn't pull out right away instead, he just sat there.

She thought she recognized him — his curly hair, his lanky features — a slim long nose and dark eyes but she couldn't place from where. So, Enaya let it go and headed into the hotel.

Enaya sat in the lobby reading her mystery novel, while she waited for her sister to return from God knows where she was. Then, she thought maybe Euly was in the shower or possibly wasn't in her room at all but decided she had a little extra time today to sit and read. The lobby stirred with bodies coming in, checking in, finding the elevator, leaving the lobby. Luggage racks wheeled in and out, the door chimed each time the sensors recognized a void splitting their connection, People talked and laughed, the phones rang for reservations or room service or the valet and there was a television set tuned to a news station for those waiting for the shuttle or taxi. The place was anything but suited for a nice quiet afternoon spent reading. Enaya closed her book and breathed out. She stuffed it into her purse and sat with her hands folded in her lap, watching the anthill of activity in the hotel.

A nervous call came down to a reservation agent. She spoke quickly and waved someone over – a man wearing a hotel nametag on the breast of his suit. The female agent hung up then picked up the receiver again and spoke anxiously to the what seemed to be another hotel employee.

"Immediately." Was all Enaya could make out the woman saying. She saw the woman roll her eyes.

The man waited next to her and they spoke in hushed tones covering their mouths. They seemed to try and break the tension with quiet nervous laughter. The man seemed to think of something and went into the office behind the counter. He resurfaced with a leather bound notebook. As he flipped through it, the woman looked on.

When the phone rang again they both jumped. She answered it then handed it over to the man. The man while still on the line signaled to the woman to make another call.

Enaya was used to the noise of the city – the early morning garbage trucks, traffic buzzing outside humming like electricity and, of course, the sound of sirens wailing in the distance. Today's siren began like a mosquito in your ear. It grew slow and with a rhythm she'd become accustom to. As it neared its sound became more frantic as if the mere closeness of it meant some unspoken doom was lurking by. When she saw the lights flashing down the road at the intersection she expected to see it streak by the window and out of sight to somewhere else. But, when it slowed in front of the hotel, she knew.

As the ambulance wheels bumped over the lip of the parking lot, the man in the car pulled out and nearly backed into the row of cars behind him. But the ambulance pulling up in front of the lobby distracted her.

She watched as the EMTs open the back of the ambulance and pull out a gurney. She watched the hotel employees aiding them — telling them the floor number. The male agent whispered something to one of the emergency people and they headed to a service elevator. Then, they were gone. The agents tried to collect their composure. They looked around the lobby at the people visiting or waiting or just plain watching and smiled at each trying to quell the worry they were seeing in their guests eyes.

"Everything's okay." The man said and pressing his hands down as if it was a room full of dogs not people.

Enaya looked at some of the people looking at the others between them, she knew it wasn't okay. Someone was either sick, injured, or worse. The busy hotel eased and people stopped talking hoping to hear something, anything of what might have happened. The female agent picked up a remote controller and increased the TV's volume. It was a signal for everyone to go back to what they were doing. The professionals were there. They would handle things now.

Enaya needed to take a more proactive stance. She knew the employees wouldn't tell her anything so she pulled out her cell phone and dialed Euly's cell. Enaya only got her message to leave her information, which she did. Her cell didn't switch over quickly like one that is turned off or already in use. It rang five times before switching to the answering service. Euly's phone was on.

After a few minutes, Enaya got up and went over to sit in a thick chair by the lobby phone and dialed her sister's room but again she didn't get an answer. When the room's phone switched over to the hotel's operator, the female agent at the counter picked up. But, Enaya hung up before she said anything. She looked over to see if the agent had seen it was her but she hadn't. At the same time, the service elevator made a sharp ping and the doors opened. There was a body on the gurney, a woman, with oxygen strapped over her face. Enaya noticed an IV in her arm. They worked fast. They rolled the gurney through the lobby fast and out through the doors. The manager came from behind the counter and followed them. He talked momentarily to one of the EMTs. Heads nodded in agreement while the ambulance doors remained open waiting for the EMTs to get in.

For Enaya, it was involuntary. She stood when the manager walked in his quick slapping steps away from the counter and toward the door. It was as if someone else were telling her what to do — to follow him and watch. That's when she looked at the woman lying on the gurney and although it was shadowy inside the mobile hospital room, she could recognize her sister anywhere.

"Oh my God. Euly!"

The man turned to the door behind him. He and the EMT put out their arms to hold her back.

"That's my sister."

CHAPTER THIRTY TWO

"Moon, what do I owe the pleasure?" Belle's, her voice filled with breathy effort and the edge of quiet anger brimming each word, didn't try to hide her sardonic tone.

"What the hell are you trying to pull?"

"I don't know what you're talking about."

"Please. Look, you sent your daughter on a wild goose chase. Why is it so difficult for you to be truthful with them? If my Micaiah was alive today..."

"Don't get all holier than thou with me, Moon. Even though you may think it, you're not perfect."

"I'm not going down memory lane with you today, Belle. I don't have time. I'm calling to tell you that you've put your daughter into such a state that she broke into my house and went rummaging through my personal things. Is that what you'd intended? These girls are all you have, all you'll ever have, and you treat them like toys. Is this the memory you want to leave them with?"

"Get off my ass, Moon. You always acted as though you were better than I was. One thing you've got to remember is that Ray left you for me. Don't you forget. He tired of you."

The silence thickened.

Belle remembered the events much the same way Moon did but neither could sort out what had transpired more than fifty years before. It had become an amalgam of different stories, his, hers, theirs. It had been told and retold so many times no one was sure of the facts any longer. It had seemed Belle's breathing stopped, something she couldn't afford, as she waited for a retort.

When Moon spoke the words flowed through the line with a pain that was palpable. "Well, maybe that's so. You need to talk to your daughter. Enough said." The skirmish ended with a click like that of a book being closed. Her ear cupped the phone like a child's to a seashell.

CHAPTER THIRTY THREE

"Are you all right, Mom?" Geoff recognized Belle's agitated state and worried for her lungs to hold out.

Belle wiped her face with the back of her hand trying to recover. "You're back." Her words whispered with jagged syllables, she looked around trying to locate the phone and to set the receiver back onto it.

Geoff stood in the doorway.

"I'll get it. You okay?" He walked over to her and took the phone and set it down for her.

"Fine. It's nothing."

"Have you heard from Euly. She hasn't called me in two days. I was wondering if you'd heard anything from her."

"No." She wasn't about to reveal any of what Moon had told her.

"I'm starting to worry. I've called her cell but there's no answer."

"I'm sure she's fine. You know how she gets."

"Yeah, but I don't like it."

"You married a writer, Geoff. They're an odd bunch."

"You can say that again."

"If she calls me I'll let you know. Likewise, honey, if she calls you first, let me know. Deal?"

"Deal. So, how are you today?"

"I've been better. Today it's my heart."

Artis came in, grabbed Belle's wrist, found a pulse and looked at her watch. She counted to herself, made a mental note and patted Belle's hand. She smiled. On the computerized chart she keyed in the information and reviewed at a tape that had printed out on one of the monitors.

"You feelin' okay, honey? You spiked a little."

"It was nothing. I just felt a little anxious."

"Okay. You let me know next time you start feeling a little anxious. We can help with that, you know. It's a medical center." She smiled with her red-painted lips and soft round eyes. "Okay. I'll leave you two alone." She winked at Geoff.

"Anxious?"

"It's nothing."

He knew Belle, if she closed the subject on something you didn't dare bring it up again.

"You need anything, Belle? I can run out and get whatever you want."

"It would be nice if you would get my drawing pad out of my closet there, dear. It's up on the second shelf."

"Sure thing."

When he opened her closet, a wave of Belle's scent wafted out and it stopped him. He stood unmoving for too long. His throat caught and his eyes burned.

"The second shelf, dear. Don't you see it?"

"Yep. Right there." As he reached up he

wiped his eye on his shirt sleeve. He couldn't let her see. He coughed once. "This one, right?" He held it up over his head without turning to her. "Anything else?"

"That should be it. My pencils are here in my drawer."

He closed the closet and Belle's scent was enveloped in the antiseptic stark odor of the hospice.

CHAPTER THIRTY FOUR

She wanted it.

He knew she wanted it.

She had egged him on like she did so many years before. He felt foolish to have fallen for her again.

Clive fumed as he stormed out of her hotel room. He pressed the elevator buttons in a rapid-fire motion as if he were knocking on a door. When the doors opened an Hispanic maid no more than twenty years old with a cart of cleaning supplies tried to push out. They nearly collided.

He rolled his eyes and motioned with his arm a little too hasty for her to go first. She said sorry, sorry in broken English and rushed to get out of his way. He pressed the buttons inside with the same rapid-fire action and when the door closed he heaved out a sigh but the elevator stopped at the fourth floor. He barked out in anger and slammed a fist onto the wall before the doors had a chance to open. When they did, three younger men wearing swim trunks and t-shirts who were talking and smiling, got on.

They talked about the evening before and about the girls at the bar. They stressed the word "bar" and, for Clive, he understood it to mean, an exotic dance bar.

When the elevator stopped again on the second floor Clive became undone.

"Dammit!" He didn't care there were other people inside the elevator.

The men stiffened and became quiet. He rubbed his head and neck.

"Hurry the hell up." He pressed an older couple entering the elevator. A lead silence hung in the air as they all watched for the doors to close. One of the young men looked at another one and nudged him but the other guy shook his head at him as if to say, don't say anything. When the doors opened Clive pushed between them before any had a chance to get out of his way.

"Nice." The younger guy taunted. It was the one who'd been nudged by the other.

Clive's gait slowed but then he decided to ignore him. He didn't care. The guy was the least of his worries. He stomped hard against the tile as he walked until finally making it out the hotel's doors.

The warm air hit him like an oven. It refreshed him.

He pulled his keys out of his pocket when he approached his 1984 Camaro. He had trouble getting his key into the lock. He was still feeling the booze. When he made it inside, he flipped over the engine. The sudden blast from the air conditioner blew out a parched dust into the air that made him breathe in a quick breath and cough.

He reached over to the glove compartment, opened it and pulled out a flask. He unscrewed the cap and took a gulp. Metal against metal made a familiar scraping noise and his mouth watered. He sat for a second against the hot leather of his chair and took a drink, then another.

As the air from the vents turned cool he nursed the flask once more before setting his head back onto the head rest. He screwed on the cap to the flask and dropped his arms into his lap.

He replayed what had happened with Euly —

the slut. He felt used but she'd gotten the information she so desperately needed. He started to laugh and then faded into oblivion.

It was the siren woke him. With the flask still balanced between his legs and the car still running, he blurred awake. A string of drool snapped when he sat upright. He wiped his mouth and took one more slug of liquor then put the car into reverse and backed out.

CHAPTER THIRTY FIVE

"I'll tell her, Geoff. She'll call you when she can." Enaya slipped her cell phone back into her purse. She dropped the cigarette and smashed it out with her toe. The pavement where she stood was scattered with cigarette butts from others who had stood right there, like Enaya, possibly calling family.

It was getting close to dinner time. She looked high above the hospital wall to the sky but only saw a smattering of blue through a haze of smog.

She knew her sister would smell remnants of cigarette on her but she didn't really care. She had good reason to smoke today.

The hospital's entrance was surrounded with thick oversized concrete block. The block etched in cartoonish figures reminiscent of *Kokopelli* dancers with flutes some heads in the air some pointed downward. Enaya blew out the last remnants, puffs of white, evidence of the cigarette. Jimmy despised her smoking. She'd taken after her father and mother. Some shit just can't be undone.

Nurses were still milling around Euly when she walked back into her room. They caught each other's eyes, her sister's with a look somewhere between fear and embarrassment.

The accidental overdose of oxycodone mistaken for aspirin, felt inadvertently intentional to Enaya. Looking at her sister there, in a hospital gown, with fluids draining into her arm, made her eyes burn. She tipped her head to the side and jutted out her bottom lip. Tears filled Enaya's eyes slowly.

Euly's shoulders moved up then down and she sighed. Tears rushing out, brimming up and over her bottom lids.

"We'll be back in a few minutes to check on her." One of the nurses, the one in-charge, warned Enaya.

Enaya made a movement with her head that she understood and moved further into the heart of the room. The others finished their business and walked behind Enaya to leave them alone but left the door open. Euly tipped her head in a way that meant her sister was to do something.

"The door."

Enaya closed it behind her then walked over to the bed. Standing, at first, Enaya grabbed her hand and leaned down to kiss her cheek.

"You had a cigarette."

"Hush."

Euly wanted to explain for a second time but began to cry. Enaya grabbed the box of generic tissue available on every table in every hospital room and handed it to her.

"It's okay. Don't get upset again." She sat down. "Look you've had quite a day, huh. Want some water?"

"I think I've had enough!" She chuckled nervously.

But, she took the water and drank it in one go, gulping loudly. When she finished, she breathed in and out in shallow gasps.

"I couldn't move, breathe. It was terrifying."

Her face contorted and her chin began to quiver. "You're okay. You're okay, now. Don't think about it all right? You shouldn't get excited again.

Have they given you anything? For your nerves?" She shook her head 'no' and rubbed her arm.

"Oh, Enaya. I'm such a fool." She gulped in a pocket of air and held it so she wouldn't start crying again and instead moaned. The humming of it resonated against her closed lips.

"Hey. Settle down. Just breathe. And, don't say that. I'm the only one allowed to call you a fool." Enaya smiled trying to take her mind off whatever was troubling her.

She shook her head quickly in agreement and tried to smile. "Does Geoff know?" She choked out the words.

"That you're in the hospital?" Euly nodded.

"Well, yes! He's worried. He said you didn't call him yesterday or today."

"Oh, shit." She turned her head from Enaya and brought fingertips to her mouth.

Enaya reached over, tapping her hands lightly. "Don't. Your fingernails look like hell as it is."

Euly dropped them from her lips and turned her head away.

Enaya opened her bag and raised an emery board. "Ta da!"

Euly turned to see and smiled. Enaya grabbed her left hand. "Hold still." It was a sweet and gentle order. The filing relaxed Euly.

"I don't know anything anymore, you know?"

"Ah, the great unknown. What do we really know, Eu? If we're lucky we might, at some point, feel like we know ourselves but I'm telling you, even that's sketchy." Her sister continued to file and finished with her pinky nail. She patted her hand and made a gesture, asking for the other one. Enaya enjoyed playing the older sister role.

The residual effect of the drugs, softened Euly's face. "Tired?"

"Yeah."

"I'm not going anywhere. Why don't you rest."

"How boring."

"Darling. You're nothing like boring." Enaya chuckled. "Get some sleep. We're in this one together."

Enaya continued to file her sister's hands. And, as Euly drifted off, Enaya tears flowed freely.

CHAPTER THIRTY SIX

When she woke, Enaya was still there, as promised, sitting next to the bed and reading a book. Enaya hadn't noticed Euly awaken.

The sky had turned into violet. Through the window, Euly could see the sun bouncing off the tip of a distant office building. It yellowed the walls and sparked off its windows.

"What time is it?" Her words startled Enaya away from reading.

"You're awake. Uh, it's close to seven p.m. How do you feel?"

"Sleepy."

"Yeah, you crashed pretty fast."

"Enaya. I want to tell you what happened." She closed the book and held it on her lap. "Do you remember Clive and Sandy?"

"That's who that was!"

"What?"

"I saw him leaving the hotel."

"Oh God."

"What was he doing there?"

Euly paused. Her face changed.

"What did you do?" Enaya's question darkened.

"Oh, Enaya. I'm so ashamed."

"Did you have sex with him?" Her voice arced with accusation.

Euly needed more time, to think, to recover.

She pressed the button to lift the head of the bed. She adjusted her body into a sitting position and rearranged her sheets. She grabbed her water cup and sipped.

"Look, I'm not going to lie to you. What I did was wrong..."

Her sister expelled a long breath of air and scolded her with her eyes.

"What I did was wrong but I didn't sleep with Clive. Christ Enaya. Will you give me some credit here?"

"Okay, then, tell me what happened?" Euly explained why she met Clive that first time at Benny's. She explained her reasoning for the follow-up meeting. Then, she continued to tell Enaya how she let him believe she might sleep with him, as she put it, for the information she needed to get out of him.

"But, I didn't, sleep with him, that is. You have to believe me, Enaya."

"So, what happened when you got to your room?" It wasn't a question but more a command.

"He was stalling. He wanted to, you know... do it first."

Euly made a face as if she'd swallowed a fly. "God." She shuddered. "I told him I needed the information first. It went back and forth like that a few times and then he asked me for a drink, you know, from the mini-bar. I poured us a couple drinks and, I'll tell you Enaya, he was already half in the bag. I mean, even if we had tried to, you know, I don't think he could've gotten it up."

"Gag."

"Sorry. Anyway, when I handed him his drink he grabbed my arm and pulled me down onto the bed and on top of him. I struggled to get off but he held me in a lock and all the while was pawing at me and groping. Then, he flipped me over onto the bed. He was on top of me! His entire weight pinned me." She rubbed her face with both hands. "It was awful. I thought, oh my god, I'm gonna get raped!" Euly's eyes plated open, stunned, then she went on, "I couldn't breathe. You know, I don't know how he did it in his condition either but he locked one arm around my waist and, oh dear Lord..."

"What?!"

Euly rolled her eyes, shaking her head as she spoke. "He dry-humped me, Enaya." She put both hands onto her cheeks and shook her head quickly. ""He had an erection." Her face bent as she spoke. "I think he came in his pants."

"God. I think I could've gone my whole life without hearing that."

But, Euly wasn't amused. She stopped for a second and looked down. "I don't know. I could be wrong but he seized up and everything. God. It makes me sick to think about."

Euly waited for a second gauging the look on her sister's face. "It got worse."

"Please. Lord."

"He tried to tug my pants off but couldn't.

He was so drunk. He was breathing and slobbering all over me and trying to kiss me but I kept turning my head from side-to-side, saying, 'Clive, get off of me. Get *off* of me!' I began to kick and scream. I think I nailed him in the groin. I'm sure I did. He crumbled onto the floor next to the bed."

"Then, he left?"

"Yeah, but not before he told me what I wanted to know, at least, I think I wanted to know. I don't know now. Maybe he lied. He was pretty pissed at me."

Euly paused and looked at Enaya who rolled a hand at Euly intending for her to keep talking. "What did he tell you?"

"See, that's just it. Maybe you know and have been keeping it from me." She watched Enaya's face to see if she was hiding the truth, if she had been all these years. "Do you?"

"No! I have no flipping clue. What it is? Tell me."

"Oh, Enaya, this is huge." Euly's eyes opened wide making her sister's open wider also but then Enaya's darkened.

"Cut the drama, Eu. Just tell me."

"Remember, we believed that dad's indiscretion was with Sandy?"

"Yeah."

Euly paused too long for her sister and Enaya huffed out her impatience. Then, Euly's face went slack as she remembered. "Wait. Oh, God. Oh, yeah. I have to back up a minute, sis. Let me first tell you this. Before I left home, mother had told me something. I don't know why she said it. Maybe it was intended to lead me off the scent or something. Or, I don't know. Maybe, now that I think about it, that's not it at all. Maybe she wanted to tell me the truth but couldn't and blurted out something else that seemed more plausible to me. I'm not sure." By this point, she was sort of talking it out to herself and wasn't really speaking to Enaya.

"What are you talking about?" She had become agitated with her sister's rambling.

"Sorry. Well, just before I came here. In fact, it's why I came, really. We found a photo while we were going through her albums."

"The one you showed me."

"Right. The one I showed Clive too. She reacted, Enaya, to the photo. She reacted as if she'd seen a ghost. I know that sounds silly but it's true. She wanted to tear it up."

"Okay."

"Well, she started to tell me something but then stopped. I prodded her on, told her not to worry, that it couldn't be that bad. You know, the things you say to people so they'll open up."

"Yeah."

"Well, she hemmed and hawed until I couldn't take it any longer and after I'd pressed her, and I pressed her, sis. I just didn't let up on her. Poor mother." She faded into a pain that Enaya could only see.

"Go on, Eu."

"Well, she finally caved in and blurted some ridiculous story out about Micaiah."

"Micaiah? What about Micaiah?"

"She told me that he was our brother." She stopped talking, watching her sister's expression — to see if she might know. Euly raised her eyebrows in a prompt but Enaya shook her head as if she were clueless. "That dad and Aunt Moon had had sex even after everyone was married and Micaiah was the product of it. Did you know any of this?"

"Not at all."

"I don't know. Maybe she really believes it but I don't think so, not after talking with Aunt Moon."

"You talked to Aunt Moon about it?"

"Of course. I had to know."

"You had to? Euly, is there anything you don't have to know? Is everything your business?" Enaya couldn't believe her sister's gall.

"Do you want me to tell you what happened, or not?"

"Boy, you need therapy."

"Who do you think you're telling?"

"Go on." Enaya seemed to give up and slunk back into her chair.

"She was incensed."

"Who?"

"Aunt Moon. Track, Enaya. Try to follow me here." Enaya rolled her eyes at Euly. "So. You're not going to like this next part. I mean, if you didn't like the part where I broached the subject with Aunt Moon, well, you're really not going to like this much either.

"What?"

"Well, the door was opened. I mean who leaves their doors unlocked like that. In Phoenix, no less."

"What are you talking about?"

She began to raise her hand toward her chin. "I just filed those. If you chew on them, I'll kill you." Euly dropped her hand. "Now, what door was open?"

"Her garage door. And, well, her kitchen door."

Again, Enaya rolled her hands for her to keep talking and sat forward.

"I went into her house when she wasn't there."

"You did what? Euly. For crying out loud."

"...and I found Micaiah's birth certificate."

"What!"

"I can barely believe it myself. Oh, and boy, was Aunt Moon pissed off."

"No kidding, Eul."

"Well, needless to say, she threw me out."

"Oh my God."

"And that's why I didn't call Geoff."

"That was yesterday?"

"Yes. So, as you can see, my stay in good old Phoenix has been quite eventful. Plus, after giving it a lot of thought I've decided I'm not cut out for detective work."

"Euly. You've really screwed the pooch."

"I don't need a lecture, Enaya."

"You think this is funny?"

"Of course I don't. I'm telling you because you're my sister not my preacher." Enaya sat back in her chair and raised both arms, sort of surrendering and for Euly to go on. "But, what I've just told you fades in comparison to what Clive had in store for me. No sir, sister, his story is quite different from the Micaiah lie. Quite different indeed."

"Get on with it." Enaya just shook her head, allowing her sister to drag out the inevitable build and the final telling of her pronouncement.

"Okay. So, I told you how I felt that mother had blurted the story about Micaiah because she wanted to put me off the track or something, right?"

Enaya nodded.

"Well, after Clive had got off of me..."

"Please."

"He was furious. He said, I'd led him on, which I did sort of and it was wrong but that's what happened."

Enaya flipped her hand again in quicker circles for her sister to continue.

"So, after he'd gotten off of me he began to scream. He called me a slut which, apparently, he doesn't understand what the word slut means or else he wouldn't have called me that. He could've however called me a tease or something else but certainly not a slut."

Enaya rolled her eyes.

"Anyway, it wasn't dad but mother." She stopped talking abruptly.

A tall hefty nurse clad in white – white cap, white uniform, white stockings, white thick shoes – walked in. Euly looked up surprised when she entered the room.

Enaya's eyes squinted. Euly's opened wide as she returned her sister's gaze.

"How ya' doin' sweety." The tall nurse asked.
"Better."

"Need anything?" She tipped the blue plastic pitcher toward her to look in. "Water's okay, huh?"

"I'm fine."

"Good. Hungry?"

The thought of food led Euly off the subject she and her sister had been discussing. "You know, I think I am starting to get a little hungry."

"I bet you are. When did you last eat?"

"Why, I don't remember. Maybe this morning. Oh, yeah, an apple."

"How 'bout you, miss. Would you like to stay for dinner? Your sister's paying." She chortled and grabbed her waist.

"I don't care." Enaya's comment sounded rude and she ignored the nurse. "Finish the story."

The nurse straightened her back and let her arms hang in surprise.

"Enaya." She glared at her sister.

"Sorry. Sure. Whatever." She waved the back of her hand at the nurse, not looking at her but instead staring at Euly.

The nurse held her chin up a little higher. "I'll be back in about a half-hour." She walked out and looking hurt.

"That wasn't very nice."

"I don't give a damn about her. Get on with it."

"Where was I?"

Her voice sounded as if Enaya was holding back a storm. She rolled her eyes. "You said, 'It wasn't dad but mother.'"

"That's right."

She waited to see if Enaya would get it through all of the diversions and her roundabout way of getting out the information.

Enaya squinted showing Euly that she wasn't sure.

Euly lifted her eyebrows in order for her to think longer on the subject.

Enaya tilted her head like a dog will when you tell it, "Treat!"

Euly pressed her eyes open, as if communicating the words telepathically.

Then, she thought she detected a glimmer of understanding from Enaya.

It was slow. Like a shadow lifting. As though someone pulled a paper bag from off her head and, finally, allowing her to see.

"What are you saying?" Enaya pressed.

"Come on, Enaya. Don't make me."

"It wasn't dad but mother?"

Euly nodded twice and lifted one side of her mouth. "Yeah."

"The indiscretion?"

"Yeah."

"Mother and...?"

"Yeah."

"Sandy?"

Euly made a grimace that looked like a zipper stretched across her face. "Yep."

She watched her sister go through the steps she'd gone through earlier that day — the same steps that ended up putting her into the hospital where she now lay.

"Need a nurse?"

"Not yet."

"I have it on tape. I have it all on tape."

"What tape?"

"My recorder."

"You have to destroy it."

Euly wasn't sure about that. She lifted her eyebrows and looked to the window.

"Euly, you have to destroy it."

"Maybe. We'll see."

CHAPTER THIRTY SEVEN

After Enaya left, Euly watched people in the airport some passing her in one direction and others crossing the other way. It was the earliest flight out. Her sister spent the night with her at the hospital and then drove her there.

She was happy her sister stayed with her.

They had time to talk and laugh, to think and reflect on the past – to reminisce and sort out lies from the truths – but end the end they really weren't sure.

Euly looked at her watch. It was five-thirty and the sun was beginning its crest far off over a raised mesa that looked as if it were being held up on a cake stand. The desert had a charm. Wisps of clouds trailed red along a perimeter of sky and reminded Euly of one of Belle's paintings. Toward the north, she could make out the slightest form of the praying monk on Camelback Mountain.

An aroma of coffee filled the morning. She swirled her cup and watched an eddy bursting with cream build in its chocolate-colored center.

She looked up and watched a 747 taxi up to the accordion gate outside the window. This town was too familiar, too close, and all she wanted was to get home.

CHAPTER THIRTY EIGHT

She walked into the house. A bouncing barking, belly-aching dog ran straight into her leg, his way to greet her. When she bent down to pet him he began his pogo-stick-routine. How can you beat that kind of love but, then, she imagined Geoff acting that way and thought, I'd have to buy a gun.

"Calmly, Jonathan."

"He knows you're here when the birds start chirping." Geoff called from the couch in the living room. When she walked into the room, he looked over his shoulder at her and away from the golf tournament he was watching. She watched the control display shrink as he turned the volume down. The TV droned like background noise. She couldn't help feel a pang of disgust pool out of her and onto the floor. It seemed nothing had changed in the week she was gone.

"The birds chirp all day long and the dog barks all day long." She shuffled through some mail and saw she had another obit request.

"Jonathan, mommy's in a bad mood." Geoff channeled his comment through the dog which irritated her more. Then, he turned back to the TV and began to talk about Tiger Woods' performance that day. Nothing seemed different from the day she left. He went on about golf as if she gave one shit. She'd managed to carry in all of her luggage in one trip but now was paying the price. Plus, the dog was still jumping for attention and pulling at her purse and bags adding extra weight and stress on her spine.

"Get down." She barked at the dog. "Jeez, Jonathan. Give mommy a break."

"How do you feel?" Geoff didn't move from his spot.

"Okay. Want dinner?" By now she was hungry and inspecting the cupboards for a quick fix to quell her churning gut.

"What do you have?" He didn't hear how his question handed over accountability to her.

"What do I have? I haven't been here in a week." They danced around the problem but still spiraled toward it.

"All right. Stop. You just got home. Can't this be pleasant?"

Euly stopped pulling food out of cupboards and stood stiff with her back turned to him.

"Salmon, chicken breasts, and filet mignon."

"Is that all?"

"Those are the entrees, which do you want?"

"Well, what's with them?"

"Vegetables, salad, rice – the usual."

"No potatoes?"

"No, Geoff. You're diet doesn't include them. Remember?"

"But, I want them."

"Too bad."

"You're nice." He smiled and turned his attention from the commercial. He got up and came into the kitchen. He put his hand on her shoulder. "I missed you."

"I can't do this right now. Let me get my bearings." They'd managed to hit an uncomfortable snag and it wasn't smoothing out anytime soon. It was one of those things you hear people talking about how marriage isn't easy and you'll have times when you wished you weren't married at all. She wanted to be left alone. She'd only just gotten home and she wanted to be alone.

"What's this?" He pointed to the form for a new obit.

"New dead person needs text." She opened the package of salmon and placed it in a glass dish.

"Nice."

"Yeah, it pays the bills."

"No, I mean the "new dead person" comment."

"Oh. Sorry. The newly deceased human being needs me to write a glowing obituary for him."

"Good lord, Euly."

"What? Do you want me to get emotionally involved with each person who needs an obit?"

"I guess I just expect a little more compassion, that's all."

"Compassion is for friends and family members." She didn't really mean any of it but was saying it nonetheless. "Look, I treat the surviving family with the utmost respect and concern. You'd think you'd know that by now since this is the way I've been making my living since before I met you." And, just like that, they were back into the snag.

"You wonder why I watch golf."

"Well, you act like I'm not nice to these people. I am. You'd think I could be myself with you every once-in-a-while. Can't I? With you? I mean, you are with me."

"You're not as open about that either sometimes."

She put her hands onto the counter and looked into the sink. It was dirty from a bowl of cereal, a spoon of peanut butter and a plate with mysterious yellow particles crusted onto it.

"Look, let's drop this. I got another job, period. That makes," she counted aloud and on her fingers, "five from last week, this one makes six and it's only Wednesday. If this trend continues, I can take next week off and work on things that I want to work on."

"Wow."

She looked up at him to see if he was jibing her or if he was being serious. Her eyes flickered as they measured his face.

He must have sensed her doubt. "No, really, Euly, that's great."

"This one is for seven-hundred words with links and two photo inserts. I'll bill close to seven hundred. The others I'll get out this week are all around six hundred. That's close to three thousand dollars this week. Pretty good, huh?"

"Yep." He paused.

She turned to him glowing with pride and assumed he was thinking about her run of fortune when he continued, "I wish we were having potatoes."

His sudden flip to the unrelated topic made her anger flare up fast. She would have a record-breaking week and he wanted stupid potatoes.

"Yeah, well, we're not. We're having rice."

Steamed rice, she thought.

Everything thing he said or did lately angered her. She felt like getting out of it once and for all.

The refrigerator reeked of something dead — something rank. Geoff caught a whiff of it too. He commented how awful it was before ambling back to his spot on the couch.

She'd been home less than an hour. She was amazed the ray of anger she beamed into the back of his head didn't explode his skull right then and there, but it didn't.

He remained oblivious there in front of the big screen as he watched a little white ball make its way across another distant golf course green. She envied him, the way he could escape to some other place in his mind, some refuge. She couldn't without packing suitcases and buying an airline ticket.

She squeezed half an orange over the salmon and sprinkled on salt and curry pepper as a marinade. Then, she drizzled olive oil over it and turned the pieces of fish dredging them in the juice. While she prepared dinner she remembered, she was protected. The property was hers from the last failed marriage. The prenuptial agreement made sure of it.

CHAPTER THIRTY NINE

The sun was setting behind a thick bank of clouds. Belle had a resolved air about her. Her time had been used up, her secrets revealed. Sadness no longer held her life in check. Her lungs did. It was more a sense of closure that Euly detected in her mother's voice. She spent this moment with her mother watching her, watching for signs of her dying.

The air was unmoving and crisp while they sat under a scrawny-armed elm out in the courtyard. It was obvious Belle had taken a downward turn.

She could see her mother struggling for oxygen. Euly thought they would've had longer. She hoped until the spring.

A dark cloud billowed and filled the sky. It seemed so near she felt she could reach out and grab its thick cotton boll. And the scent casting off hinted of snow, not rain this time, snow. She thought, you could tell snow was coming every time – thick with salt as if the ocean itself froze and sent its messenger, telling everyone to go in for the season and rest, to pull over a thick quilt and sleep. This winter's message was one Euly wanted to postpone. She wanted time to freeze there as they sat together outside in the cold. She looked away from her mother and breathed in deeply.

"It's frosty."

"Are you too cold, mother?"

"No, it's nice, it makes me feel alive." Euly didn't respond. Belle had earned the

right to say what she felt even if it upset Euly. She closed her eyes and pressed her chin to the sky.

"I spoke with Enaya yesterday. We had a nice long chat."

"That's good." Euly opened her eyes and wondered what the conversation was between them.

"She'll be here tomorrow."

"What time?"

"She should be here in the morning, early."

Euly looked at her watch. Night was coming on. "She's getting a rental car and will come directly here to see you, okay?"

"Okay." Her voice was quiet as if she didn't mind one way or the other.

"You know, mom..."

"Euly?" Belle interrupted. "Have you ever wished you can turn back the hands of time?"

"Boy. Let's see. I can't count that many times on my arms and legs, fingers and toes."

"One thing I've learned is mostly things happen for reasons. But, if there was ever a time in my life that I could change things, it would only be so I could spend more time with you girls. Not to change outcomes. Does that make sense?" Euly looked over at her mother but Belle continued to talk before she could respond. "Try not to judge yourself to harshly dear. It's simply not worth it." Then, Belle looked directly into Euly's eyes. "Will you promise me that, Euly? Promise me you'll go easy on yourself?"

Euly grabbed her mother's hand and, holding it to her face, began to cry. But her mother wasn't done.

"Be good to your sister, Euly. She'll be all you'll have of our little family after I'm gone. Find it in your heart to be good to your sister. She loves you so much, honey. Do you know that?"

Euly nodded that she understood her mother and wiped her nose. "I know mom."

"By the way, young lady, how did you become so critical?"

Euly shook her head knowing her mother wasn't finished.

"It's a waste of time." Belle paused for a several heartbeats before she went on. "Love your husband." She breathed in and out. "He's a fine man." She breathed again. "Quite a catch."

She squeezed Euly's hand and continued in a whisper. "He has been here... every day... since you left... quite a catch... that one." She paused and struggled in another breath. "He brings me things... Like I need things..." Her eyes glistened and she smiled. She patted her daughter's hand.

Her final stream of whispered words showed Belle's unusual strength at this point. "He doesn't know what to do with us. We Masada women are tough eggs, you know? He doesn't know what to do with you." She looked at Euly and took in air. "Look at me, Euly." She meant to drive home a point by putting one finger under her daughter's chin. Euly let her do it and when she looked at her mother, she noted how her eyes looked like an old dog's, fogged over and glassy.

Euly nearly choked her own breath.

"He doesn't know what to do with *you*." She whispered hard. "Try to understand he's just a man. They don't think like women. Our minds are always on high alert, always going in all different directions, all the time." She tapped her head with one finger. "They don't get us. You have to be kind." Belle paused, put her hands to her heart, gasped once but then relaxed back into her chair. "I can't talk anymore. Okay?"

She smiled but blinked with heavy lids at Euly. Euly mouthed the word *okay.*

"Mom? Can I ask you something about what you told me?" Just as Euly asked, Belle became unsettled and seemed to struggle for air and then began to cough.

"Mother, are you okay? Mom?"

But, the cough persisted to the point that Euly had to call for a nurse. "Mother, I'll be right back with help." Euly ran into the hospice. Her voice echoed through the halls as she screamed for a nurse to help her.

CHAPTER FORTY

Had she ever wished for anything this hard? Once. She thought maybe one time before but the wish felt distant and unattainable. So Euly dropped it like a feather and watched it drift off until it was out of her mind. They were making her *comfortable* now, as they put it, adjusting her sheets and pillows, wiping her down with warm wash clothes, swabbing her mouth and putting a rolled towel under her neck to keep her chin up so she could breathe easier. The clock was speeding out of control.

"She's sleeping now. I'll be home later when I know she's stable. I don't know when that will be, Geoff. If it's too late, I'll call, okay?" Artis came in to check on Belle. Euly ended the phone call with Geoff.

"She seems quiet now, darlin'." She tried to reassure Euly. "She gave you quite a scare didn't she, honey?" Euly nodded and continued to watch her mother. She's been having these fits for the last few days but you wouldn't know that would you, now? That sweet husband of yours, what's his name again, Geoff, is it? Well, he was very helpful. He stayed two nights, when she was particularly bad, until morning. Yes sir. He's a fine man. Good lookin' too. My, my he sure is. He's got the entire second and third shift in a tizzy. He's a good one. The girls been flirting with him. But, why not, right? The man is fine. See, the other night your mama was coughing to beat the band, she was. He fretted about her. You could tell."

"He didn't tell me."

"No, I suppose he didn't. He's not like that, now, is he?" Artis continued to check the monitors, prop Belle's pillow, tug on her blankets and check her catheter as she talked to Euly. "Now, look. Your mother is doing just fine, right now. If anything changes, I'll call you. Why don't you go home and get some rest. You'll do her no good at all if you don't have some energy."

"Thanks, Artis, but I think I'd like to wait a little while longer."

Artis patted Euly's shoulder and looked consolingly at her. "If you need anything, you just ask me, okay? Pillow, blanket, anything. Are you hungry?"

"No, but thank you."

Artis looked at her and tipped her head. She went to a cupboard and pulled out some bedding. She set it on the recliner.

Euly could see Belle's condition was getting bad. They'd aspirated her lungs. They put her on an IV and intubated by inserting a tube down her throat to supply the oxygen she needed to breathe. Artis left momentarily but came back in with a syringe.

"What's that for?"

"Something to make her sleep better, darlin'."

"What is it?"

"Morphine, honey."

"Morphine? You can't give her morphine, it will kill her!"

Artis looked at Euly with a deadpan face. "Who ordered this?" But Artis' face didn't change. "Tell me! Who ordered this?"

"Honey, your mother asked when she got to this point to give her morphine so she wouldn't feel any pain."

"When she got to what point?"

"Honey…" Her voice trailed off with a lilt intended for Euly to understand, like she was supposed to 'get it.'

"What! It's not time yet. She's not dying. My sister isn't coming until tomorrow."

Artis set down the syringe and faced Euly and grabbed both her hands but Euly pulled away. "No. You can't make this better by coddling me. You can't do this."

"Euly." Artis grabbed her hands again and Euly broke down. "Honey. It's what your mother wants. It's between her and God now."

"It's not supposed to be this way. She's supposed to stay longer."

"Shh. Come on sit down." Artis helped Euly back to her chair. "You know, let me tell you something. In all my years here at Madrona Gardens, I've never met a more amazing woman than your mother." Euly nodded her head. "She loves you girls so, do you know that? She brags about you girls day and night. She tells us you're a writer, that you're writing a book or something. Is that right?" Euly nodded again and then looked over at her mother. "And your sister. She sounds like a dear woman. How many kids does she have again?"

"Three."

"Three kids. Ain't that the best? She a good mother?"

"She's a great mother."

"Takes after your own, does she?"

"I suppose she does."

"Now see ain't life funny, darlin'? She always told me you were the spittin' image of her." Artis looked deeply into Euly's eyes and nodded her head.

"She used to tell me that I was just like dad."

"Probably a little of both, don't you suppose?"

"Yeah. I guess so."

Artis grabbed Euly's chin so she would look into her own eyes and smiled.

"Oh, Artis, why is this so hard?"

"It always is, honey. It always is." She stood up straight and cocked her head at Euly. "Now, let me do what your mother wants."

"Can you give us a few more minutes together? Five minutes, Artis. That's all I ask, just five more minutes."

"Of course, honey. I'll leave you two alone."

CHAPTER FORTY ONE

"Did I wake you?"

His voice scratched out the word, no. "How's she doing?"

"Not well." She couldn't talk.

"Honey, I'm sorry. Do you want me to come?"

She sniffed before speaking again. "No. No, it's okay. Come in the morning. Early."

"Are you sure? I can come right now."

"No, honey. You need your sleep. Artis told me."

"She needed company. It was no big deal."

"It was huge."

CHAPTER FORTY TWO

When she woke up an orderly was checking the drain bag. Its scanty level of urine rose up only an inch from the bottom. He keyed in the amount on the Belle's chart and walked out. She rubbed her eyes and looked at the clock. It was a quarter after three in the morning. Her mother looked content lying there in bed and Euly wondered if she was smiling. She sat on the edge of the bed and grabbed her mother's hand.

"Mom." The first time was quiet. "Mom."

The second time she tried to revive her mother was louder but ineffective and she wouldn't awaken so she yelled to her. "Mom!"

It was no use. Belle was unresponsive. She put a hand to her mouth. She looked around the room for help. She stood then she sat. She stood once more and went to the phone and dialed her sister. Euly got her answering service. "I don't know where you are, sis, but if you can you need to hurry."

She hung up still watching her mother lie there. Belle seemed thin and weak — thinner than she had before Euly left for Phoenix. She felt a wave of guilt flood her body and she sat down and reached out for her mother's hand.

"Mom, remember those games you used to play with us? We had fun, didn't we?" Euly laughed as if her mother were whispering a joke into her ear. "Yeah, remember those treasure hunts? Weren't they a blast? You had us going for hours looking for little gems, up the stairs, in the bushes, under pillows, everywhere! We didn't need TV when we had you. You were so smart. You knew what you were doing – sending us off in search of a token or something, keeping us busy so you could paint. You know, mom, you were everything to us. You were the best." Euly put her head down on the bed by Belle's arm and cried but stopped and wiped off her face. Her mother still smelled like she always had – a mix somewhere found between *Jergens* and that indescribable but distinct essence of Belle. Euly thought for a moment she could make out a trace of linseed oil but dismissed it, figuring she was playing tricks on herself, tricks into imagining it. She pulled back Belle's covers and sat on the edge of the bed. It felt firm but soft. Then, she slipped her legs under the sheets and laid on her side next to her mother. It felt familiar and natural. She wrapped her arm around her mother's waist and whispered to her. "Hey. I just want you to know all that stuff about Micaiah and Sandy. It means nothing, you know? I don't care. I understand now, mom."

CHAPTER FORTY THREE

She didn't hear Artis come back in. "Honey?" Artis woke her. It was five thirty.

"Oh, yes." Euly sat up in the bed and tried to gather herself.

"This will only make her sleep better, honey. She'll hang on for a little while longer."

"But, my sister's not here."

"She shouldn't become agitated at this point honey. I have to."

Euly cupped a hand over her mouth as Artis injected the drug into the IV's drip line. When she finished she looked at Belle.

"There darlin', sleep well my friend." She looked up at Euly. "I'll miss her too." She nodded and then walked out.

It was then and there Euly realized how many lives Belle must have ed. She wished, at some level, she could've been more of a friend to her than a daughter. She wished that she could've been more mature in accepting her, like Aunt Moon, who would listen to her stories and not judge her, and even if she did, she wouldn't say — that sort of friend, the very best of people, someone who would just listen.

"Mom." Euly whispered now. "I'm sorry for not being there for you. No, no. I'm not talking about now, I'm talking about then when you might've needed someone to talk to. I know you don't need any apologies, but I want to give you one, okay. Just let me, this one time. Okay?" Euly was holding her own conversation with her mother as she laid there unconscious.

She needed to call Enaya again.

CHAPTER FORTY FOUR

Euly's head rested on the bed but she wasn't asleep. She heard the desperate steps from down the hall approaching Belle's room when Enaya raced in. Euly lifted her head off the damp on the bed spot and turned to look at her sister.

She couldn't stop her chin from quivering.

Shook her head. "It's over."

"Oh God, no."

"I told you to come as soon as you could. Where were you?" She looked at her watch but it was only seven. Belle had hung on until only moments ago. Euly began to cry.

"Eu, I just couldn't get here. I'm sorry. Let's not do this now. Okay?" Her sister walked over to see their mother.

Euly looked at her. She looked weathered and older today, harried and unkempt.

"I'm sorry, sis." Euly held her hand out for her. Enaya walked in stolid steps over to Belle and grabbed her hand. She squeezed it once and then let it go. She bent over and kissed Belle's forehead.

"Mom," Enaya paused and then whispered. "I tried so hard to get here. Really I did."

"She knows."

Euly stood and pressed closer to her sister. She grabbed Enaya around the waist and pulled her closer. Enaya turned into her face into Euly's shoulder and cried. It felt odd, her older sister always weakened when dealing with family issues. Somehow Euly realized her sister's weakness grew out of fear. She couldn't face the pain and so Enaya hid, escaped, ran away from to distance herself from the torture and grief. Euly remembered she had done it when their father died. She patted Enaya's back and squeezed her tighter.

"Enaya. I told her you would be here and here you are." Enaya buried her head in her sister's shoulder and they stood by Belle, the three women of the family together again. Then, she lifted her mother's covers. "Come on. Let's get lie next to her one last time."

CHAPTER FORTY FIVE

They filled out all the necessary paperwork and collected the last bit of their mother's belongings. They were zipped up and handed to them in a large plastic see-through laundry bag. Geoff showed up and helped them get most of her things for them.

Euly held the bag. From what she could tell, it contained the clothes her mother was wearing when she passed, a notepad and pens, her slippers and a silver chain holding a key. While she scanned it she wondered how many people had done the same thing in this very spot. She looked at the floor where she stood.

"Is that it then?" Enaya handed back the papers she'd signed to the administrator.

"That's all. We're so sorry for your loss." The woman's standard dismissal moved Euly and Enaya away from the desk and down the hall. Euly wanted to offer a snide retort but halted. What else could the woman say? It was just a job to her. She was probably a mother herself, thinking of her own children, wanting to finally go home.

Even so, it felt funny leaving for the last time. Euly figured she'd miss the place and her visits there.

Enaya and she didn't speak until they got outside.

"I'll follow you home."

"Okay."

The two women hugged each other longer than normal then broke away and walked to their cars. Euly noticed a young boy and his mother walking toward her. He had a small nosegay with silver and gold balloons attached. It had bright pink cartoon lettering reading, Happy Birthday, Gramma! The boy chirped away asking his mother a question and she gave him in what seemed to be the standard response, her answer. "Yes dear." She ignored him for the most part as they passed. The woman stared at the doors to the hospice without a trace of emotion. Euly stopped and turned to watch her while she pushed the boy along with one hand on his back. His small feet worked double-time to hers. Her right hand was hoisted in the air, keeping her purse slung into the crotch of her elbow. Steps away she heard her say again in her robotic tone. "Yes dear." She continued to hum and repeat as they walked until they entered the hospice and disappeared inside.

The sun was battling clouds low in the morning sky and the air was damp with mist. Euly

turned her face to the gold rays. It felt warm while the mist filled the every thread of her clothes and sending a chill sweeping over her skin and making it pop. A shiver ran down her back.

When Enaya beeped the horn, Euly jumped.

She put her hand to her chest and took in a breath. Enaya lifted her hands in a question. Euly rushed to open her car door, tossed in the plastic bag and said, sorry, to her.

CHAPTER FORTY SIX

Excitement seeped in for the first time since their mother died. Euly felt it bubbling up as they decided where Enaya would sleep.

"You'll be more comfortable there at Mom's. We won't be bumping into each other. You can poke around in all her stuff. I have. You'll have fun."

"I don't know. You won't mind?"

"Why would I mind?"

"I don't know. I wouldn't want you to think I didn't want to stay with you."

"Did you ever consider the possibility we don't want you to stay with us." Her ribbing went unappreciated.

"Well, I kind of want to."

"Want to what?"

"Stay at Mom's."

"You should. I've been through her stuff so many times I've lost track. Besides, when was the last time you were here." She watched her sister as she tried to remember the year. "Stay at mom's. It's really sweet."

Enaya smiled. She seemed to get a little giddy about it.

"Come on. I'll get one of your bags. Why did you bring two suitcases? Where did you think you were staying, the Hilton?"

"Shut up. I always pack like this."

"It's just a week."

"Drop it."

"A week, Enaya, not a month."

"Okay. Okay."

CHAPTER FORTY SEVEN

The house was bright even though the sun had now been consumed by thick low-hanging clouds again. It was a time of year when the sun could not be relied upon.

Enaya opened the door. She was happy when her sister mentioned it first.

"Oh my God. That smell."

"Isn't it great."

"It smells just like mom."

Enaya dropped her bag in the doorway partly blocking Euly. She padded her way into and through the cottage like a kid entering Disneyland. She walked over to the rustic wooden stairs leading up to the loft.

"She climbed these?"

"Up until she moved into the hospice although I think there might've been about a week where she stayed on the couch. But, yeah, she climbed them." Euly pushed the bag with one foot into the house and closed the door.

"Jeez. Look at this place."

"I know."

Enaya grabbed the makeshift rope railing and stepped onto the first step. She climbed with her head angled upward staring dead ahead. "Ohmygod." She said it out loud but hadn't intended it for anyone else but herself. Euly smiled. She understood her sister's anticipation. She hadn't been there in four years, not since the fight. There were ghosts up there.

"I'll make some tea." But Enaya didn't answer as she walked up the stairs.

Euly pulled out two of her mother's favorite teacups and the pot that matched them. She ran hot water into the teapot. The water clanged against its metal bottom until it reached a deep enough level. She placed the pot on a burner and remembered the gas needed to be lit with a match. A long red lighter was next to the stove on the counter. She flicked it on and held it to the burner. It belched out a flame that subsided as quickly as it had lit. She adjusted the setting to high and went to the cupboard where Belle kept her tea. Squatting down to see, she spotted five hand-painted tins with labels each marking the blend within – Earl Grey, Paris, Green Mint, Orange Spice and English Breakfast. Euly decided to treat her sister to the Paris blend this morning. It was the one Belle had told her was for special guests. She didn't think she'd mind this one time and who could be more special than her sister right now, right there.

The tin bloomed out a fragrance that wafted up in sweet tones of vanilla and jasmine when she opened the lid.

"Oh God."

"Are you all right?" Her sister called down from the loft.

"Fine. Sorry. This tea is haunting."

"She was amazing, huh?"

"Yep." She wanted to tell her she had missed a lot but didn't. It wasn't necessary.

Enaya's footsteps creaked above her head and she smiled. It reminded of visits to her mother's in the past when Euly would help herself to her favorite tea then. It was as if her mother were still there. The thought stopped her in her tracks until she hear her sister coming back down the stairs.

"Wow. How many boxes did you guys pack."

"Oh, several." The pot hissed lightly where a light stream of steam escaped. It jiggled from the water inside as it began to boil. "Tea's almost ready."

"Mm. It smells delicious. What is this one?"

"Paris."

"Uh-oh. Mom's best blend. Are you sure we should?" Enaya sounded like a kid.

"Hmm. I don't think she'll mind. I don't think she ever minded really."

"She went a little crazy in here didn't she?" She laid her hand on the design their mother had painted on the walls.

"I don't know."

"It seems she's painted every hard surface in the place."

"Well, yeah. So."

"Stars and moons. They're everywhere."

"It was her cosmic stage – her universe stage. She would tell me, 'Keep positive vibes flowing out to the universe and they'll flow back to you threefold.' It was as if she were excited about dying. She somehow welcomed it. Does that make sense?"

"Well, she sure seemed to suffer there in the end."

"Maybe. I don't know. Maybe not. She had a smile. Did you see?"

"Yeah." She blew on her tea. "The colors in here are so cheery. You'd be hardcore to get depressed in this place."

"Her house was her biggest piece of art. She loved this place. I mean, she loved Phoenix too, you know, the warmth in the winters but she thought this place was the closest she'd ever been to Heaven."

"Well, it looks as though you're right again. I'm going to love staying here."

"Can you stay longer than a week?"

"There's work and the kids."

"The kids are teenagers, Enaya. Anyway, aren't they staying with Jimmy's parents?"

"Yeah."

"Do they do okay with them?"

"Oh God. They hate to come home after being there."

"Would his mom and dad be okay if you stayed a little longer? God knows you packed for

it."

"Shut up. I don't know. We'll see."

"There's a small washer and dryer upstairs in the loft. You'd never be without clothes."

She shook her head but smiled at her sister's teasing. "I'll check with Jimmy when he gets here tomorrow. It would be nice. Anyway, he doesn't have to stay longer if he doesn't want, right? I mean, he could go home and take care of the kids for a few days without me. Right?"

"Right." She grabbed hold of her sister's hand and squeezed.

"I'll see what I can swing."

"I sure do miss you Enaya. It would be so great to have some time together after the funeral."

"Well, like I said, I'll see what I can swing."

"We have a lot to do tomorrow."

"It's not going to be fun."

"No."

CHAPTER FORTY EIGHT

Dreams from early morning were more like visitations than dreams. She'd had them before but none so crystallized or succinct with people and surroundings as in this morning's dreams. The "visitations" were as if people came to her in the nighttime lying there suspended in her semi- hallucinogenic state seeming more like cameo appearances by old dead actors from black and white movies. But, once awake, they remained in Euly's head as though she'd just turned off a movie with the plot dangling in her memory and fixed in her subconscious long after it ended.

It all started with a dead friend calling her. Her ex-husband was there. He answered the phone and said, "Hold on, hold on, she's right here." It seemed he needed to scream into the phone. When Euly grabbed the phone her voice echoed loudly into the mouthpiece, "This is Euly!" She was yelling too over the din of television noise in the background.

"Hello! They're holding it for you right now!" Someone said on the other end, but the blaring noise of the TV made it impossible for Euly to hear him.

"Hold on, I can't hear you. Will you repeat that?" Euly covered one ear.

"They're holding it for you." He repeated. "Wait, oh I'm sorry Andy, but it's loud in here. Let me walk into the other room." But she walked outside instead. "Okay, there. I can hear you now." And as clear as day, she was talking to her friend who had died two years before.

"They're holding it for you."

"They're holding what?"

"They're holding a spot for you." And although the conversation was

disjointed, Euly understood. When she thought

about her dream later, she knew the dream was about life. It was interesting to her that the message was delivered by a dead friend and lacked a sense of foreboding.

The morning's dream stayed with her as she heated water in the microwave, as she steeped her tea and added her creamer, and as she sipped it and curled into the arm of the sofa. The clouds rolled in and rolled out skipping across, covering and revealing an iridescent blue sky, stealing then offering each spotting breathlessly. No matter what, days continued to fall off the calendar. Time, she'd heard, heals broken parts of hearts. Still, as clouds passed through and her days would step further away from these moments, the pain remained as it did that millisecond, in their final moment together. The moment they held each other one last time, took that one last breath together. And, she knew she merely existed in a daze of days.

Tears streamed whispers down her cheeks. She wondered when the well would run dry, when she'd no longer find herself going under in a pool of tears. It was a two weeks before Thanksgiving. She always felt sad around the holidays but this season would be sadder because their mom died yesterday. She hoped her sister would stay with her longer than she'd planned to.

Euly asked Enaya if she wouldn't mind if she wrote the obituary. Her sister agreed that she could. Her first task of the day however would be a simple act, an act that seemed to overwhelm her just thinking about. She needed a shower.

Later, Enaya and she were to meet with the mortician about funeral arrangements and, after that, they were to visit the priest. If they had time, they would begin selecting songs and photos and decide on cards and flowers and needed to make a list of people to whom they would send announcements. The day was already full but Euly was thankful she had help — her sister was there with her.

She cleaned off a spot on her wooden library desk. It sat in the center of a lovely large bay window that looked out over a sprawling grassland behind the house. The swale led to an area that had become a refuge for animals near the pond about three hundred yards off in the distance. In the early morning it filled up with deer, raccoons, fox, eagles, geese, mallards, and the occasional snoopy mink. The days always seemed to start out this way, foggy and misty, and lazy and it seemed that's how they ended too.

This day, however, the fog hung thick over the pond, whipping cream thick, in clumps like ice cream floating in a punch bowl. From her view, Euly thought she knew what Heaven might look like, what it might feel like.

But, then, she felt weak. Her stomach quivered and her jaw tightened. The desk was covered with paper, papers about dead people. One was a man who'd died in an auto accident who left behind an aging wife, four children, and seven grandchildren. Another was a child who died of leukemia — her family found it important to mention her love of movies about Dracula and had only one best friend. She left behind her grieving mother, father, sister and brother. Another was a woman, a wife and mother. She died of breast cancer. Her children were barely teenagers.

Euly wondered why she did it, why she wrote obituaries. The practicalities were valid – the money was good, but why obits. Was it a sense that reading about other people's death made her feel alive? She wasn't sure anymore. She wasn't sure about anything except that she had to write her mother's obituary today – now before her shower. Everything else would wait.

Euly sat down and stared at a blank page that blinked on the computer. She rested a pair of reading glasses on the bridge of her nose. She angled her head up to see the words then down so she could see farther off. She sat with her hands in her lap. The screen pulsed, anticipating her words. She heard the whirring of the disk spinning inside its chassis. Nothing came to her.

She gazed over toward her mother's cottage. The wooden sign Belle had painted swung lazy in a soft breeze and dripped from the wetness brought in by the fog.

Art is Life, Period.

Belle had painted the words in big bright crimson letters. It hung on brass chains above her door that squeaked when it was windy. Euly imagined the noise it was making now as she sat at her desk watching the sign quake in a light rhythm and seesaw in the morning's wind.

Bird droppings trailed down in a line under the eave from swallows of springs past and looked as if tears down a clown's face. Her mother had gone so far as to buy mealworms for the birds. She'd attached a dish close to a window so she could watch the birds eat.

Euly smiled when she thought about that day — about the ladder that leaned against the wall and Belle balancing on a rung as she reached over her head swinging a hammer. She wore a leather tool belt with a loop that held the hammer. It had a pocket for nails that snapped close. It was odd to see her aging mother still doing the things she used to do when she was younger.

"Mother, what are you doing?"

"Putting up a bird feeder. I have swallows!" She was so excited when she said it and Euly remembered her thinking her mother was crazy.

"Swallows can ruin your eaves."

"Well, then when they leave, I'll fix the eaves. No harm. No fowl! Get it? No fowl?"

And, Euly responded in an overly casual tone,

"Yes, mother. I get it."

But today, Enaya was there, inside Belle's home, possibly rising or having coffee, reminiscing or preparing, possibly crying. She never understood her sister — never got her — how she removed herself, how she stayed above the action of family business. She wondered if Enaya was that way with her own children or if they weren't subject to her submerged emotional state. But mostly Euly wondered if they too would perpetuate that same sense of reserve and coolness so prevalent in her sister. When she thought back, she couldn't remember if Enaya was that way when she was younger or if she'd developed it after she'd gotten older.

Then, a memory struck her as if she'd been shot through the heart, it was a recollection of the party, the one in that photo. Parts of it flashed in her head like a slideshow projector – their family's metal-framed pool, their father digging by hand a hole twelve feet in diameter and three feet deep, Uncle Teddy and Clive helping him and using every care necessary, and Aunt Moon with Sandy and Belle serving food and supplying the men with refreshments. And the careless coffee stain.

The men kept their eyes on the kids and warned them not to get too close to the hole. Their childlike minds wandered once again to the games they were playing. As the men struggled long and hard into the dark they'd finally finished digging, to fit the metal siding along the perimeter of the hole, just to pull it out again and correct it. They were tired and hungry but refused to give up the task until it was done. There'd be no tomorrow working on the pool. After they'd gotten the siding into the hole the next step was simply a matter of back-filling in dirt around the edges to stabilize the structure, after that they would hang water-blue nylon lining inside

it and, finally, fill it.

Nearby, the kids were laughing, Micaiah was stuffing an entire hotdog into his mouth just to see if he could and, he could. Enaya and Euly roared as they ran in circles around him. He was chasing them with part of the bun hanging out of his jaws. Then, something went wrong. She'd lost track of where

she was running and wasn't paying attention. Euly

remembered slipping. Her foot slid between the metal siding and the edge of freshly dug hole. She'd been warned but couldn't stop her body as it fell into the siding, folding it in on one side and creasing the metal.

Her father went ballistic. He yelled at her in front everyone and she remembered crying and running inside. She remembered Enaya screaming back at their dad, defending Euly and running after her inside to console her. They'd been a team once. They had been close.

Yet, as they grew they were two branches

splitting a tree at the bole growing outward and away from each other. Enaya had a way of distancing herself, walking outside a margin of family dangers where Euly would step waist deep into the quicksand and end up sucked into its pull.

And, there she was in mother's cottage, a place Euly hadn't ventured since a week after Belle moved into the hospice over five months ago. Now, her sister was deep in it and for the first time in a long time and Euly was the one circling, not ready

to deal with the realization that her mother was

gone for good. The woman who hummed lullabies to her as she rocked her to sleep, had left for good.

The phone's bell startled her. Her heart raced

in a start. It was eerie to see Belle's name lighting up the digital display, like some celestial beacon

glowing from another plane of existence. She wiped off her face.

"Hi." She whispered, covering to hide the sound of crying. Her sister spoke with morning in her voice. Enaya wanted to know when she would be coming over. She wanted to make breakfast and it was ready to go and she could put it on the stove right now and, no, she didn't care if Euly wasn't

ready.

"It's not like your neighbors will see. You're socked in by woods. You're so uptight. How did you get like this?" And, in her statement, Euly got the sense that Enaya also thought about how differently they'd both turned out from one another, how the spread seemed abysmal and out of reach. Yet, her sister was only feet from where Euly now stood, within yelling distance. Euly turned to the window looking out to see if she could spot her sister but she couldn't.

"Is that your idea of an invitation, an insult to wet my appetite?"

Enaya smiled. She could hear it in her sister's voice. "Just come over. We can have coffee together and eat. Then, we can look for it."

Enaya wasn't a patient woman. She'd never been patient. Euly knew this. Enaya — always the first up at Christmas, the first done with a math test, the first to move out of the house, to move away, to move back — the first born.

"Okay. I'll be right there."

As she hung up the phone, she looked out to the frozen pond and could see rings of water that had once beaten against its edges and trees now stiff from icy temperatures. Willows bent under pressure of cold air. She could feel winter seeping in.

CHAPTER FORTY NINE

After her grandmother vanished the diner filled-up with performers – actors, singers, and musicians. They begged Euly to dance.

"I don't dance anymore." She told them but they prodded and pressured her to get up and dance with them. She rose up and with one quick move, a step from long ago, Euly said, "Like this?" The performers cheered and applauded to see her aging body move.

She dreamt she awoke in the dream and found she was in bed alone. A very small and frail version of Belle crept into the room and up to the bedside. Euly began to quake and moan as if she were seeing an apparition. She awoke once more in the dream but her mother was still there this time trying to console Euly. She said, "You were crying in your sleep."

"But mom, you were just here by my bed." The distorted version confused her.

"No, I've only just gotten here." Then Belle yelled out, "Honey!" Someone else was standing behind her. It was Euly's father.

"Honey, Euly thinks I was here beside her bed, but I've only just gotten here, right?"

"That's right. Hi honey." Then they both tried to console her.

She jerked in a start when she woke. The grief felt unbearable.

Euly had the overwhelming feeling that she was swimming in quicksand. She'd drifted off. The phone was ringing again. It was Enaya. It was still morning. Had she missed breakfast? She remembered coming upstairs to wash her face and brush her teeth and had only intended to lie down for a spell.

Euly wondered her mother heard her when she was lying there unconscious. If the dream wasn't Belle answering her from a place where people can only communicate through dreams — that's what some Native Americans believed. It seemed plausible now. And, in Belle's unconscious state — that place somewhere between sleep and death — Euly wondered if people had an ability to hear and comprehend words spoken to them. She hoped so but would never know.

CHAPTER FIFTY

Their mother had always maintained the upper hand with her daughters and now her sister seized the role with ease. It was some odd pecking order like in the animal kingdom but one never spoken of on any TV shows or reading Euly could recall. Enaya took charge where their mother had left off and now she was in her house. It amused Euly to watch as she transformed from the woman

she was only yesterday to this newer version. Maybe spending the night in Belle's home did it.

"I waited as long as I could. Here. They're not as hot as they were an hour ago." Enaya wasn't smiling. She dumped a thick pile of cold eggs onto each plate. Placed four slices of stiff bacon down and poured orange juice into two small pink juice glasses.

"Sorry, I fell asleep." She scooted in her chair under the egg-blue table. The wooden legs screeched against the wooden floor.

"Whatever." She stuffed Euly's last comment in with all the other worthless excuses she'd heard over the years and sat down. "Coffee?"

"Sure."

"Well, I'm not the maid. Get up and get it."

"Yes ma'am." Euly fetched the coffee pot and brought it back to the table. "Want a refill?"

"Don't set that on the table. It'll burn."

"It's a thermos. It's not hot."

"Oh."

"Yeah. I got it for her a while ago. You can sit them anywhere, take them too."

"Sorry."

"You didn't know."

"No. I mean sorry about the 'maid' thing."

"Mom used to say that too." She smiled at Enaya and her sister took a breath.

"I'm not good at this sort of thing."

"Who is?"

"You are."

Euly reached over and grabbed her sister's hand. It felt soft and weak. "You're doing fine. We're both doing the best we can. I know one thing for certain, though."

"What's that?"

"It's time for me to grow up."

Today was a mix of emotions. She had received another award, an award this time for an essay she hoped to fit into her memoir. Euly was always amused by the randomness of timing and decided to wait to tell everyone until dinner. Dinners with family all sitting around a table were times for happy news. Jimmy would arrive later today and meet up with Enaya. Family would be together.

Geoff left early for golf. He was still hurt, hurt about the Clive incident. She could see it in his eyes. Still, she knew he was getting over it when he wanted to make love this morning. It was the first time in two months. Both of them were being tender to the other — Geoff was because of Belle and Euly, because of Clive.

The dog and cat were fed, the litter box cleaned, a load of laundry in the wash. She wanted to feel excited about the award but couldn't work up the strength. She knew today would be filled with old memories.

The letter read...

To my most beautiful daughters:

Look for the red star in the heart of my world. It is locked and safe near the well-read dhurrie with three boards from the setting sun. The red star holds answers to your questions about life.

One day, you'll understand we're all children at heart with dreams and hopes, loves and desires, and memories of a time way back when...

Miracles happen. Look in the mirror.

I love you both more than life.

I won't ask for forgiveness because I've lived my life fully and with zero regrets.

I'll love you forever, your mother. 5/3/1976.

CHAPTER FIFTY ONE

The instructions were locked inside the a thin nondescript envelope and Euly held it like the Holy Grail as she made her way to see her sister. Wind blew her hair into her face. The air was crisp but the clouds and fog were lifting under the sun's power. Fat clouds still skipped by in-between sun appearances spotlighting them as if actors walking from entrance to exit across a stage, adding to their importance. She kicked the door, knocking it with her foot.

"Why didn't you just come in?" Enaya frowned but Euly didn't answer. She only stared at her sister in dumb amazement. Her sister bent forward to her and brushed the hair out of her face. "What? What is it?"

"The last one." She opened her eyes wide.

"The last what?"

Euly cocked her head as if to say, come on!

"Treasure hunt, you dope."

"No shit." Enaya's eyes softened and her jaw slackened.

"No shit."

"Get in here."

She grabbed Euly's arm and pulled her into the cottage.

They sliced open the seal with a letter-opener they'd found in the loft at her desk and carefully unfolded the note from inside the envelope. They flattened a map out over the kitchen table and read their final instructions.

"She painted the floors for our benefit."

Enaya pointed to the reference of a red star noted in her letter to the girls.

"That stinker."

Euly thought back on the week it had to be done.

"Mother can't this wait?"

"I can't wait. I'm not going to be around much longer. It has to be now."

She held a hand to her mouth and started to cry. Enaya rubbed her back. "Unbelievable."

"She just had to do it. She wouldn't take no for an answer."

Her sister went into the bathroom for a box of tissues. When she came back she was wiping her own nose.

"Here. I think we're going to need these. What do you think?"

"Oh yeah." Euly laughed a little.

"Okay, little sis, let's figure this one out." It was more than an hour later when they discovered it — a loose split in the floorboard. It was nearly invisible and looked like just another seam in- between the wooden slats. They looked at each other.

"How do we get it up?"

Enaya rubbed the floor searching for something, any irregularity. "Here it is."

Euly rubbed over the same spot. "Oh lord." She let Enaya have the honor and, when her sister slipped her index finger into the middle of the red star, it gave way and made a small hole. She pulled up. The secret panel lifted out easily. The hiding place was a foot deep and housed a two-tone brown and black leather satchel with two buckled straps that, when connected, kept it closed. There was also an old-fashioned brass lock in the middle to keep out the curious.

"Get the key."

Euly jumped ran to the counter near the envelope where she'd left it and raced back with it held out.

"Here."

Enaya wore no makeup this morning and yet her cheeks were tinged with blush.

"Oh my God." Euly felt her heart race as she watched her sister move closer to the satchel.

She unlatched its buckles one by one and when she placed the key inside the lock she looked up.

"Ready?"

Euly took a deep breath in and opened her eyes. "I don't know. Wait. *Wait*. I'm not sure we should do this."

"You're getting cold feet now?"

"Just… wait a sec. I can barely breath."

"That's because you keep holding your breath. Breathe."

Euly took in two deep breaths and looked at her sister. Her sister raised one eyebrow.

"I can't help it. I'm nervous."

"Oh, for crying out loud."

"Dad used to say that."

"I can see why."

For Euly, the click sounded like a small bomb exploding and when the lock dropped open, she felt herself jerk. Enaya didn't ask if she could remove the lock off nor if she could lift the lid of the satchel.

But, she did. Inside was filled with stacks of paper each held neatly together like a present with jute twine wrapped around crossways then lengthways and finished off with a small bowtie. The stacks were made up of letters inside envelopes, folded drawings and photos.

"I wonder who they're from."

"Let's look." The finding emboldened Enaya but made Euly shrink. "Over here. I'm tired of kneeling. Let's move onto the couch." They pressed up from kneeling on the hard floor and stood with a grunt from the exertion.

"I remember a time we didn't make as much noise doing the same thing."

"Yeah. We also had about a hundred and thirty less pounds on us. Come on."

"Speak for yourself."

"Shut up. I meant on us, together." Enaya elbowed her sister. "I was only kidding." She hoisted the satchel and walking it over to the couch placed it in the middle. Euly sat on the opposite side. "You first." Enaya smirked at Euly.

"You stinker." She studied the contents. "Most of these are to mom." She picked the pile closest to her and held it up to her sister.

"Go on."

She pulled the string to the bow that held her pile together while balancing it carefully in her hand as she unraveled. Enaya grabbed a stack but raced through the string. Some of the letters fell onto her lap. Euly's were still neat and orderly and she opened the topmost torn envelope and pulled out a letter. "Whose handwriting is this? It's not dad's. Is it?" Euly held it up in front of her sister's face. She backed up Euly's arm so she could read.

"Doesn't look like dad's." Enaya examined the outside.

"Oh no."

"What?" Enaya rushed to open her letter. "These are from Sandy."

Her sister hurried to get the letter out that she was holding. A thin strip of silk periwinkle cloth dropped out, fluttering onto Enaya's lap.

"What's this?"

"It looks like mom's scarf."

Both read quietly. When they were done, they swapped.

The photos were of Sandy and Belle together in most cases but she had contained in the trove a few pictures of the girls when they were babies, toddlers, adolescents and teenagers. The drawings were of Sandy of her face and of her nude.

"This makes it real, doesn't it."

Enaya breathed out a sigh but didn't speak. Her lips pressed together and tipped up on one side in a sort of disapproving look.

"They loved each other. I mean, these letters, they're pure love."

"It's too weird."

"Maybe. She was scared. She lived a lie and for how long? Could you do that?"

"To the very end? I don't know."

"She was brave. She didn't have to tell us at all. We would've always wondered if Clive was lying. The truth would've died with her."

"I kind of wish it had."

"Come on, Enaya. She's trusting us, with one of the most important stories of her life. And, you know what?"

"What?" She rolled her eyes.

"Listen now. Don't be like that. I know it's a little freaky but that's for two reasons — one, we're straight and, two — she's our mom. It wouldn't be weird if she weren't. But, this is the thing here, the way I see it is that we have a choice."

"A choice."

"Yeah. A choice. We can either tell people or..."

"We can keep her secret."

"That's right."

She gauged the changes in her sister's face. It transformed in steps. Her eyebrows lowered in a squint. She tilted her head to the side. Her eyes softened and she smiled. Not a wide smile a knowing smile like how you feel when your head breaks through from under water and you get that first breath of air.

Euly wondered if she'd ever seen her sister look as lovely with her hair still tumbled from sleep and in her lazy flannel pajamas. It came back to her, a long ago memory of her tearing through presents under the Christmas tree. When Euly held her hand open to her, Enaya grabbed it and squeezed.

Coffee should be black as hell, strong as death, and sweet as love. [Turkish proverb]

CHAPTER FIFTY TWO

With Geoff still sleeping, Euly snuck outside onto the balcony. Leaning her elbows on a blue plastered balustrade, she cupped her *kahweh baida* in both hands warming them against the thick bone ceramic of the mug. She waved her nose above the brew taking in hints of cardamom and goat milk cream amid the strong coffee scent.

When she looked into the mug, cream spun and fused into a silky bronze homogenate after stirring in the honey. She left the spoon sitting lazy inside the cup. It seemed to be waiting for her, like a cocky boy at the prom.

After a brief but hard morning rain, a bed of creamy apricot blossoms had fallen and blanketed the lane that ran below their hotel room in the quaint village. Geoff's plan to come to Lebanon in April had been thought out to its most finite detail.

He wanted everything to be perfect and it was. Euly knew how hard he'd been working to fix whatever had gone missing between them. There, in JBail she felt an unfolding of love, resurrected again, light and glowing as if from a renovated ancient papyrus, somewhat discolored but completely legible. It felt for her like the first moments when she and Geoff had met--real, pure, and true.

The cobbled road below their room drifted off somewhere close to the coastline and reminded Euly of a long bridal path. The image took her back to their wedding six years earlier back home, under a 60-foot tall noble fir in their yard. A brisk wind scudded up and lifted with it a scent of ocean, the smell of salt and kelp hung there with her in the balcony before filtering away.

This place--so different in culture and atmosphere--felt natural, felt homey.

A lone church bell knelled off in the distance across the small village, distracting her. She lifted her head in the direction of its tolling. As the clapper swung and see-sawed clanging a message through the air, it made the moment crystallize, and stop in time--a snapshot in her mind.

The tinkling of an unseen chime startled Euly, drawing her attention across the other way. When she turned her head in the sound's direction, a young teenaged girl appeared wearing earphones and low-slung jeans peddling her bicycle from around a bend of the village's main road.

The relic of a bike she wheeled toward the hotel down the narrow strip of cobbled brick, set off how out of place the girl looked, alien with spears of bread poking out of the canvas sack in her basket.

It brought the twenty-first century into diametric view. This place still reminiscent of a war torn country from the 1970s, was expending great efforts in order to come of age in the twenty-first century.

The ivory-colored blossoms, confused by the intruder, swirled in circles behind her and settled to watch her as she rode away.

Up there on the balcony, a person could see so much more. From up high the theatre below, with its actors playing out a farce or comedy (whatever the mood du jour), captivated the audience in its acts and scenes wrought with magical anticipation.

The days, so near a new month, it was tough to call it April anymore. Euly's breath reminded her of the garlicky hummus from dinner the night before. Geoff loved lots of garlic in his food. He would say time and again, "The only way to fix a dish with too much garlic is to add more, that's what I always say." That and, "Garlic is its own food group."

Euly turned from the scene below and watched Geoff flipping through pages of Beirut's leading newspaper, The Daily Star. Steadying her spoon between a finger and the mug, she sipped from her cup and smiled. Walking back through the open set of sliding glass doors she placed her coffee on the table next to an oversized chair.

"What's happening in Lebanon today?" He didn't understand one iota of Lebanese but had learned enough to order wine and food, find a bathroom, and to get a taxi but other than that his grasp of the language was far from fluent. After arriving, they both realized the classes they'd taken and the cryptic knowledge of Arabic they had learned, was time spent in vain. Most people spoke English there. The Daily Star had been, for years, published in English.

"LaHara Com Sar eet, honey." He smiled up at me. "I am so thrilled this paper is in English." He folded the newspaper and laid it on the cocktail table. "Pretty too. Just look at all those colors." He took a slug of coffee, slid his rump deep into the wide chair and kicked up his feet onto the ottoman. "Ahh, this is the life." He closed his eyes and acted as if he was going to sleep again.

"Are you going back to sleep?"

"Uh-uh. Just closing my eyes."

"You're going back to sleep."

"I'm going back to sleep." A grin snuck across his face and trickled off through his shut eyes.

"When do you want me to wake you?" She understood their trip was meant for relaxation and fun.

"In an hour?" He asked.

"Okay. I'm going to take a walk and find a place to sit. I'm going to try and find someone to speak Arabic with." She grabbed the newspaper off the table. "I'm taking this too."

"Yeah, yeah, my little Lebanese terrorist."

"Geoff!" She made a tsk at him.

He popped one I open to look at her. "I love you."

"I'll be back in about an hour, okay?"

"Yep."

She started out the door and then called back before she closed it, "Love you too."

He smiled without opening his eyes.

CHAPTER FIFTY THREE

A mourning dove perched next to its mate and cooed as they watched passers-by below them. They hid amongst the vivid jade leaves and within what was left of any blossoms in the pear tree. She took in a deep breath taking in the perfume of the blossoms and the freshly mown grass along a meandering path on her way to the resort's swimming pool. An echo of birds answered each other and conversed in soulful and lonely calls pitching up and down in an echo across the resort property.

She heard a jogger approaching from behind and expected the person to pass on her right so she edged closer to the fringy grass along the path. But, the footsteps slowed into a fast walk.

"Hey lady, wait up." Geoff panted and bent over to grab his knees.

She beamed out a smile and then turned to welcome him.

"I thought you were napping."

"I wanted to be with you more. We can sleep later." He stood up. His eyebrows fluttered at the innuendo and she giggled.

"Doesn't it smell great out here."

"Mm hmm. You lost weight."

"Cutting back on the alcohol, all that sugar." She put her hands on her hips and swiveled this way and that for him to take a better look.

"Nice ass, Eu."

She giggled and smiled.

"Look at the blossoms, honey."

"Pretty. Did you bring your camera?"

"No. Shoot."

"You can get a photo later."

Everything to Geoff was fine if it was put off till later. He didn't like to make small problems seem too serious nor did he like to make big problems seem small. He was a perfect balance, she thought.

"So, do you think we'll make it?" She kept her eyes focused in front.

"What do you mean by make it?"

"You know, for the long haul."

"I hope so. We'll have to always remember our wedding vows."

"Yep. This is marriage, right?"

"Yep."

"That's what I used to tell myself the last time."

"Try to concentrate on the positive."

His attention shifted to a group of golfers playing on the resort's course. He'd completely forgotten the subject.

"Is the lobby the closest place with a bathroom?"

"Yes."

He put his hand up behind her head. She looked at him.

"Golf balls." His explanation made her understand he was protecting her. He had his other hand up behind his head also. "I hope we don't get hit."

"That would hurt."

While they walked she talked to him about some of the flora and fauna of the desert landscape. The Mediterranean lie just steps away from their resort with a surrounding desert that was not much different from the higher deserts of Arizona. As she noted the different varieties of cacti, trees and grasses, birds, spiders and reptiles, Geoff listened on. It appeared he enjoyed listening to her talk about fire ants and the roadrunner she'd seen yesterday dashing its way through a shrub.

"We used to go hunting with dad, for dove and quail. He liked mourning doves because they have a lot of breast meat."

Geoff made a grunt. He remembered hearing about the story before but Euly went on anyway. "He'd bring home bloody sacks of birds."

This time she elaborated. "Enaya and I would have to sit outside in the backyard to clean them." She paused and wondered if she should embellish. "Have you ever cleaned birds?"

"No."

"We'd have to rip the feathers off."

"You clean fish by gutting them."

"You clean birds by removing their feather but also by pulling their heads off."

"Christ."

"I know. We had to clean them. Mom wouldn't do it and I don't blame her." They were quiet for a few steps and then she went on. "They'd make a chirping noise because their voice boxes were being split in two."

"Man, Eu."

"I know. It's sad."

As they approached, an invisible cloud radiated and hung by the door of the resort. It was a blend of eggs, bacon and fresh baked bread. Geoff made a straight line into the restroom. Euly poured two plastic cups of ice water the resort made available to its guests. Today they layered the water with ice, blueberries, and ice again. Yesterday it was oranges. The tall tubular urn of glass and brass was sweating in the warm day's air. Nice , she thought. She wondered if Geoff would like something similar for their kitchen.

As Geoff exited the restroom, he made eye

contact with her. His eyes sparkled blue and she felt her stomach flip. She handed him one of the cups of water. He drank it down without stopping for a breather.

"It's good today."

"Blueberry."

"Mmm. Pretty too."

"Should we get an urn like this for the house?"

"That's a good idea." He took another sip that finished off his drink. "Want breakfast?"

"Yeah. That would be nice."

CHAPTER FIFTY FOUR

She slid the keycard into the door's slot and they heard the familiar click to let them know it was unlocked. Geoff pulled his cell out of his pocket and looked at its display. He must've had it turned to vibrate. The morning was turning warm and the sun shone brightly through their back door, the one they'd left open. The air inside was cool and comfortable and Euly toed-off her shoes and slid them with one foot next to the door.

"Oh no." While he fiddled with his cell phone and it chirped out a warning they had messages.

"Who called?"

"Fred and Mary." He tapped the key pad and walked to the edge of the balcony where reception was at its fullest. He said to Euly over his shoulder. "It'll be nice to get back home. I'd like a little instant replay of our action on the couch." He turned with his back against the balcony railing and grabbed himself. Euly smiled and shook her head in mock disapproval. He was such a guy's guy. His wry smile reminded her how he played havoc with her in bed.

"Hi guys. It's us. You're probably still asleep.

We got your message and we're doing great." He seemed so happy being with somebody. They were so different. He enjoyed being around people and she was content staying home alone. She never seemed to feel lonely like some people do but knew that a life with Geoff would always be a sort of push-me-pull-you grappling and that each of them needed to knuckle-under at times for the other. That's what marriage was all about, anyway, wasn't it – a giving in of sorts, a surrendering of part of yourself to someone else. The concept didn't always sit easy with Euly but only lately she felt more at home with the idea. He too seemed to be giving her more elbow room.

After she moved her office over to her mother's cottage, Euly began to miss Geoff's constant, predictable interruptions. Since her mother died, she imagined life without him and it pained her. It was a physical gut-wrenching pain.

Before, she'd been locked in some internal battle that was towing her under – a battle she created quite on her own – one in which Geoff was an integral part but one he could not fight. He sat on the sidelines handcuffed, gagged and blindfolded while Euly fought on, a fight she could never win. She was a swordfighter in a mirror.

CHAPTER FIFTY FIVE

She balanced on the edge of the bed and slathered her tan legs with lotion. She put on her wedding ring and slipped on her nightgown. The brush stroke pattern of the silk looked like thousands of linden and jade leaves all crammed together. She finished and sat slumped but stared off.

She remembered her mother asking if she ever wished she could turn back time. Euly knew she had but couldn't remember when. She knew it was futile. You can't when the hands are missing. The hands are missing, she thought. Everything seemed to take giant steps away from a comfort she came to expect and love as a young girl.

The hands, brushed antique brass, fit onto a mechanism that kept the clock moving at its correct time. Her mom's clock, the one with metallic Roman numerals attached to the wall were, at that time, the latest interior motif anyone could buy. She turned her eyes away from the digital clock there in the hotel room on the night table and spun back to a time when she was eight again. Her mother's clock

was the newest thing going – hard-wired into the wall – but only for that second when she snapped back to the present. Where she could begin to live her life again.

Euly was still dealing with Belle's death which, in turn, made her consider her own mortality. Things change but, why. A deep longing made her want to lie back and sleep. Just sleep. Time was a wispy wind that blew over you and only when you were beginning to cool from it, it blew away again. You could try but you could never catch it nor could you reclaim it. Time slipped along merrily down a road and left people wearily watching it go. She thought how beautiful it must be for those people who get lost in the past, how understandable to get lost and stay lost. She fell back onto the bed and closed her eyes. She must go on now. It was her turn, hers and Geoff's.

She called to him and when he walked in, she rose to her elbows.

"That's pretty." His face brightened.

"Thanks. I want to show you something." She waggled her eyebrows in a tease.

He twiddled his back at her comment. "Sit here. I'll get it."

"You'll get it?"

"It's in my bag. Hold on."

He heard the champagne bottle pop and called from the bedroom. "I know what it is." Life seemed always to be a guessing game for Geoff. But when she returned he asked, "What's that?"

"It's what I want to show you." She handed him the flutes and set down the bottle. "Here, you pour." Euly sat next to him and unzipped the satchel. She pulled out a two-inch-thick stack of paper. A jumbo clip held it all together. "Here." She held out the stack for him to take and he quickly finished filling the glasses and set the bottle down before grabbing them from her. He quickly read the first page then flipped to the second.

"'Dedicated to Geoff Winger. My strength.'

Wow. Is this your..."

"Yep. It's my memoir."

He put his hand on the top and set it on his lap. When he looked at her she could see his eyes were tinged with redness — that struggle between crying and not.

"Don't. It's a good thing." He wiped his eyes.

"I'm so proud of you."

"Well, that makes two of us!" She laughed. "Really, though, sweetheart, I couldn't have done it without you. I mean what I say in the dedication."

"You should dedicate it to Belle."

"Well, I thought about it. But, then, I also thought, if I dedicate it to Belle then I should dedicate it to dad and then Enaya and the list went on forever. When all was said and done, I just knew. It was you. There was no question."

"I don't know what to say."

"Don't say anything. Will you help me and read it?"

"Of course!"

"Hey. Can I read you the first paragraph?"

"Absolutely."

"Okay. Oh, I'm so excited." When Euly smiled at Geoff she could see his excitement grow. She turned to the stack of papers on her lap.

Geoff sat tall with wide eyes waiting as she lifted a few sheets from the top of the stack while she searched for the proper page to start reading.

"Here it is." Her voice spasmed with emotion and when she looked back at Geoff she had tears in her eyes. He reached across her shoulder and gave her a gentle squeeze. When he did she tipped her head onto his shoulder and held it there for a second.

"I'm okay, really."

He kissed her on the top of her head. She could feel his lips on her scalp through her hair and, at the same time, she heard him take a deep breath in. It felt good to have him close.

"Mmm. You smell good."

"Now, stop it." She pulled away slightly and straightened up.

He followed her lead and clutched his hands safely into his lap. "Sorry." He winked at her and nodded for her to continue.

"Ready?" Euly took a deep breath in and held it.

"And willing." Geoff understood the depth of this moment.

She sighed out anticipation. "This is how the story begins."

THE END

"I do not want a plain box, I want a sarcophagus
With tiger stripes, and a face on it
Round as the moon, to stare up.
I want to be looking at them when they come
Picking among the dumb minerals, the roots.
I see them already-the pale, star-distance faces. Now they
are nothing, they are not even babies.
I imagine them without fathers or mothers, like the first
gods.
They will wonder if I was important." -Sylvia Plath

EPILOGUE

"The Obituary of Belle Masada, Our Mother"

We thought we'd left yesterday behind. The indigo-blue-dawn slipped sleight of hand into an amber autumn morning, the morning Belle Masada died. Rain from the evening before left a peppery tar suspended in the air from pines outside and the sachet filled the house. And, now, a crisp breeze has wafted in unannounced through an open window, by the honey-washed table where I write this and chills the elbow — a breeze that whispered, goodbye.

Another day has lifted up another sun. Lately, the sun sits low in the south and casts long shadows across still tall, yellow grass. A soft soughing of wind whispers through trees and bends branches — makes saffron leaves tumble to rest near a bank of rose bramble. The times speak of passing. The teapot whistles on the stove and takes us back to a moment, only a moment but to the memory of a wonderful life.

Someone is dancing the jitterbug — that swingy, three-quarter jig. I make out a fuzzy snapshot of me, or maybe it's my sister, Enaya, standing on mother's feet. She holds our delicate eight-year-old hands for balance. We face the same direction and pitch fro, heel back, and rock side-to- side with some imaginary partner. What is that song again? You Send Me? Yes, that's it, by The Platters. Slow enough to learn the jitterbug.

Ascension into teenage years renders rash- ridden breakouts, screaming matches, The Beatles, and questioning authority.

"Promise me you'll never have sex!" Through mother's tears she makes us swear. "Promise!"

"Okay. We promise." But as nature plays out, we let go of our promise.

Through coming years of doubt and contemplation, confusion and separation, we survive the loss of virginity and our parent's divorce.

We marry. We divorce. We remarry. Yet, the same story repeats with millions of people, unoriginally and exponentially, over and over as if on the tide, as if part of the cosmos.

Belle Masada, artist, friend and mother, was born November 3, 1922. She had an amazing life. It's well-documented on her website at www.bellemasada.com. Our family hopes you will visit this website, if you do it won't surprise us if her story changes your life, it changed ours – mine, Euly Winger and my sister's, Enaya Spadden – her daughters who survive her and who will miss her terribly.

Our last year, our best year, we all spend close together. We re-connect but a little too late and for too short of time. With her body weak and failing her, she didn't want to die but she hung on until she could stand the loss of breath no longer and, then, she let go.

"We'll see you again. We'll always be together."

"How do you know?" I see in her eyes she's afraid.

"How?" I try to explain better. She deserves that. "Because, we're family. We're tied to one another by a string called family and we'll always be together."

We're reeling in the moment of this snapshot from our past – our lips pressing hard to her forehead, our hands in hers, lying part on part off her hospital bed – and we whisper, "Mom, we'll never let go."

A LITTLE SOMETHING EXTRA – THE RECIPE FOR KAHWEH

Coffee should be black as hell, strong as death, and sweet as love. [Turkish proverb]

Coffee (*kahweh*) is a big deal in Lebanon. It's great coffee, black, strong, and takes some time getting used to it. Identical to coffee in neighboring countries and sometimes referred to Turkish coffee .It derived from the Arabica bean known as Brazilian bean.

Lebanese coffee is served throughout the day, at home, at work, in public cafes and restaurants. When guests arrive at one's home, they are invariably persuaded to stay for a coffee as a sign of welcome, no matter how short their visit.

A visit to Lebanon is not complete without drinking the Lebanese coffee, the Lebanese way.

Drinking coffee is so much a part of the culture that it is joked that a Lebanese who didn't drink coffee could lose his nationality!

How to Make Lebanese Coffee
Ingredients
- 1 cup of water (the size of espresso cup)
- 1 tsp. ground coffee

- 1/2 tsp. powdered sugar
- A pinch of cardamom (optional)

1-Pour in cold water in the coffee pot (*rakweh*) You should use one cup of cold water for each cup you are making . Add a teaspoonful of the ground coffee per cup in the water while the water is cold and stir. The amount of coffee may be varied to taste, but do not forget. Don't fill the pot too much. If you need to add sugar this is the time to do it.

2-Heat the pot as slowly as you can. The slower the heat the better it is. Make sure you watch it to prevent overflowing when the coffee boils.

3-When the coffee begins to rise up remove from heat. When foaming recedes return to heat and bring back to a boil. Repeat this procedure three times . The goal is to get maximum coffee flavor without over boiling. There should be a thick sediment on the bottom and a brown froth on the top.

Note: The amount of coffee and sugar may be decreased or increased according to taste.

Since there is no filtering of coffee at any time during this process, you should wait for a few minutes before drinking your delicious Lebanese coffee while the coffee grounds settle at the bottom of the cup.

How to serve Lebanese Coffee: The coffee is poured out in front of the guest from a long-handled coffee pot (rakweh) and served in proper cups, about the size of espresso cups, on a coffee tray and accompanied with a glass of cold water.

Usually guests are asked how they take their coffee: with or without sugar, since sugar is added during preparation, but nowadays coffee is prepared without sugar and the sugar came along.

It is quite an art to know-when to stop drinking your coffee as one sip more and you will end up with a mouthful of the coffee residue (*tefl*) left in the bottom of the cup.

So with a tiny little bit of coffee and lots of coffee grinds still left in your cup, put your coffee cup holder on top of your coffee cup, make three horizontal circles with your cup, and then with a quick movement turn the coffee cup with the cup holder upside down. This will slowly bring down the coffee grinds along the coffee cup down to the coffee holder, let the cup rest for about 2 minutes before give it to the cup reader.

A coffee cup reader, who is usually your host at home or in specialized coffee shop will read your future by interpreting the shapes and giving you advices about life decisions and problems.

Although we are far from being able to give anyone guidelines about how to read coffee grinds, as it seems to be driven by inspiration rather than science.

White Coffee: (kahweh baida or café blanc) is invented in Beirut, it means a cup of boiling water scented with orange blossom water and sugar(optional). "White coffee "is a sedative, and calms the nerves while stimulating digestion after a particularly rich or heavy meal.

Lebanese "white coffee" contains absolutely no coffee or caffeine.

Finally, whether you are drinking your coffee from a street vendor clinking cups to attract customers, a roadside van ,or a stylish coffee offering 10 different coffee blends, Lebanese coffee is an integral part of Lebanese life, and every newcomer to Lebanon should experience it and ENJOY IT.

CLARIFICATIONS ABOUT THIS STORY

Thank you for reading, Drowning. Drowning has been, to date, Susan Wingate's most autobiographical novel. She used real people as characters although their names, sexes and in some instances, personality traits have been mixed one with the other at times. Another important clarification must be made. Susan's mother is still alive at this printing (digital and otherwise) and she has remained heterosexual her entire life.

ABOUT THE AUTHOR

Amazon #1 Best Seller and Award-winning Author, Susan Wingate was born in Phoenix, Arizona to James & Amie Ajamie (a writer and an artist, respectively). Susan Wingate tried to fly at age five off the roof of their family house using only newspaper, wire hangers and scotch tape. She's been dreaming of flying ever since. Oh, by the way, she never jumped. Her mother ran out in the nick of time to stop her from take-off.

Wingate stuck to dance lessons with a more solid ground beneath her feet. In high school, she became involved in acting and joined the drama club. At seventeen (saying she was eighteen), Wingate went on a 2-month acting tour with The Robinhood Players.

In 1997, Susan moved from Phoenix to an island in Washington State. To support herself, she ran a bed & breakfast for three years and finally closed the doors soon after September 11, 2001.

In 2004, she began writing full-time. She lives on her island with her husband, one dog named Robert, fourteen cats and, at last count, eleven birds.

You can learn more about Susan Wingate by going to her website

http://www.susanwingate.com.

The *Bobby's Diner Series* Includes:

BOBBY'S DINER (book #1) and

HOTTER THAN HELEN (book #2) "A suspenseful and well-penned novel that is sure to entertain... Read on!" ~*Suspense Magazine*

Her hard-boiled mystery novel, OF THE LAW by JJ Adams is often described as Chandleresque in style.

Susan Wingate draws and paints abstracts using oil as her favored medium. She lives in Washington State with her husband and a whole bunch of beautiful companion animals.

And, remember, if you enjoyed Drowning please leave a review on the site where you purchased a Susan Wingate book.